Through the Postern Gate

A Romance in Seven Days

Florence L. Barclay

Through the Postern Gate: A Romance in Seven Days

Copyright © 2020 Bibliotech Press
All rights reserved

ISBN: 978-1-64799-967-4

TO

MY MOTHER

CONTENTS

THE FIRST DAY

THE STORY OF LITTLE BOY BLUE

"But it was not your niece! It was always you I wanted," said the Boy.

He lay back, in a deep wicker chair, under the old mulberry-tree. He had taken the precaution of depositing his cup and saucer on the soft turf beneath his chair, because he knew that, under the stress of sudden emotion, china—especially the best china—had a way of flying off his knee. And there was no question as to the exquisite quality of the china on the dainty tea-table over which Miss Christobel Charteris presided.

The Boy had watched her pouring the tea into those pretty rose-leaf cups, nearly every afternoon during the golden two weeks just over. He knew every movement of those firm white hands, so soft, yet so strong and capable.

The Boy used to stand beside her, ready to hand Mollie's cup, as punctiliously as if a dozen girls had been sitting in the old garden, waiting to be quickly served by the only man.

The Boy enjoyed being the only man. Also he had quite charming manners. He never allowed the passing of bread-and-butter to interfere with the flow of conversation; yet the bread-and-butter was always within reach at the precise moment you wanted it, though the Boy's bright eyes were fixed just then in keenest interest on the person who happened to be speaking, and not a point of the story, or a word of the remark, was missed either by him or by you.

1

He used to watch the Aunt's beautiful hands very closely; and at last, every time he looked at them, his brown eyes kissed them. The Boy thought this was a delightful secret known only to himself. But one day, when he was bending over her, holding his own cup while she filled it, the Aunt suddenly said: "Don't!" It was so startling and unexpected, that the cup almost flew out of his hand. The Boy might have said: "Don't what?" which would have put the Aunt in a difficulty, because it would have been so very impossible to explain. But he was too honest. He at once didn't, and felt a little shy for five minutes; then recovered, and hugged himself with a fearful joy at the thought that she had known his eyes had kissed her dear beautiful hands; then stole a look at her calm face, so completely unmoved in its classic beauty, and thought he must have been mistaken; only—what on earth else could she have said "Don't!" about, at that moment?

But Mollie was there, then; so no explanations were possible. Now at last, thank goodness, Mollie had gone, and his own seven days had begun. This was the first day; and he was going to tell her everything. There was absolutely nothing he would not be able to tell her. The delight of this fairly swept the Boy off his feet. He had kept on the curb so long; and he was not used to curbs of any kind.

He lay back, his hands behind his head, and watched the Aunt's kind face, through half-closed lids. His brown eyes were shining, but very soft. When the Aunt looked at them, she quickly looked away.

"How could you think the attraction would be gone?" he said. "It was always you, I wanted, not your niece. Good heavens! How can you have thought it was Mollie, when it was you—YOU, just only you, all the time?"

2

The Aunt raised her beautiful eyebrows and looked him straight in the face.

"Is this a proposal?" she asked, quietly.

"Of course it is," said the Boy; "and jolly hard it has been, having to wait two whole weeks to make it. I want you to marry me, Christobel. I dare say you think me a cheeky young beggar to suggest it, point blank. But I want you to give me seven days; and, in those seven days, I am going to win you. Then it will seem to you, as it does to me, the only possible thing to do."

His brown eyes were wide open now; and the glory of the love shining out from them dazzled her. She looked away.

Then the swift colour swept over the face which all Cambridge considered classic in its stern strong beauty, and she laughed; but rather breathlessly.

"You amazing boy!" she said. "Do you consider it right to take away a person's breath, in this fashion? Or are you trying to be funny?"

"I have no designs on your breath," said the Boy; "and it is my misfortune, but not my fault, if I seem funny." Then he sat forward in his chair, his elbows on his knees, and both brown hands held out towards her. "I want you to understand, dear," he continued, earnestly, "that I have said only a very little of all I have to say. But I hope that little is to the point; and I jolly well mean it."

The Aunt laughed again, and swung the toe of her neat brown shoe; a habit she had, when trying to appear more at ease than she felt.

"It is certainly to the point," she said. "There can be no possible doubt about that. But are you aware, dear boy, that I have been assiduously chaperoning you and my niece, during the past two

3

weeks; and watching, with the affectionate interest of a middle-aged relative, the course of true love running with satisfactory and unusual smoothness?"

The Boy ignored the adjectives and innuendoes, and went straight to the point. He always had a way of ignoring all side issues or carefully introduced irrelevancy. It made him a difficult person to deal with, if the principal weapon in your armoury was elaborate argument.

"Why did you say 'Don't'?" asked the Boy.

The Aunt fell at once into the unintentional trap. She dropped her calmly amused manner and answered hurriedly, while again the swift colour flooded her face: "Boy dear, I hardly know. It was something you did, which, for a moment, I could not quite bear. Something passed from you to me, too intimate, too sweet, to be quite right. I said 'Don't,' as involuntarily as one would say 'Don't' to a threatened blow."

"It wasn't a blow," said the Boy, tenderly. "It was a kiss. Every time I looked at your dear beautiful hand, lifting the silver teapot, I kissed it. Didn't you feel it was a kiss?"

"No; I only felt it was unusual; something I could not understand; and I did not like it. Therefore I said 'Don't.'"

"But you admit it was sweet?" persisted the Boy.

"Exactly," replied the Aunt; "quite incomprehensibly sweet. And I do not like things I cannot comprehend; especially with amazing boys about!"

"Didn't you know it was love?" asked the Boy, softly.

4

"No," replied the Aunt, emphatically; "most certainly, I did not."

The Boy got up, and came and knelt beside the arm of her chair.

"It was love," he said, his lips very close to the soft waves of her hair.

"Go back to your seat at once," said the Aunt, sternly.

The Boy went.

"And where does poor Mollie come in, in all this?" inquired the Aunt, with some asperity.

"Mollie?" said the Boy, complacently. "Oh, Mollie understood all right. She loves Phil, you know; intends to stick to him, and knows you will back her. The last part of the time, I brought her notes from Phil, every day. Don't be angry, dear. You would have done it yourself, if Mollie and Phil had got hold of you, and implored you to be a go-between. You remember the day we invaded the kitchen to see how Martha made those little puffy buns—you know—the explosives? You pinch them in the middle, and they burst into hundreds and thousands of little pieces. Jolly things for a stiff stand-up-in-a-crowd-and-all-hold-your-own-cups kind of drawing-room party; what we used to call 'a Perpendicular' in my Cambridge days. I suppose they still keep up the name. Fancy those little buns exploding all over the place; and when you try to pick up the fragments, they go into simply millions of crumbs, between your agitated fingers and anxious thumb!"

The Boy slapped his knee in intense enjoyment, and momentarily lost the thread of the conversation. The Aunt's mind was not sufficiently detached to feel equal to a digression into peals of laughter over this vision of the explosive buns. She wanted to find

5

out how much Mollie knew. When the Boy had finished rocking backwards and forwards in his chair, she suggested, tentatively: "You went to the kitchen—?"

"Oh, yes," said the Boy, recovering. "We went to the kitchen to watch Martha make them, and to get the recipe. You see Mollie wanted them for her father's clerical 'at homes.' Oh, I say—fancy! The archdeacons and curates, the rectors and vicars, all standing in a solemn crowd on the Bishop's best velvet-pile carpet; then Mollie, so demure, handing round the innocent-looking little buns; and, hey presto! the pinching begins, and the explosions, and the hopeless attempts to gather up the fragments!"

The Boy nearly went off again; but he suddenly realized that the Aunt was not amused, and pulled himself together.

"Well, we stopped on the way to the kitchen for mutual confidences. It was not easy, bounded as we were by you on the one side, and Martha on the other. We had to whisper. I dare say you thought we were kissing behind the door, but we jolly well weren't! She told me about Phil; and I told her—oh, I told her something of what I am trying to tell you. Just enough to make her understand; so that we could go ahead, and play the game fair, all round. She was awfully glad, because she said: 'I have long feared my dear beautiful Aunt would marry an ichthyosaurus.' I asked her what the—what the—I mean, what on earth the meaning of that was? And she said: 'An old fossil.'"

Again the swift flush swept over the calm face. But this time the Aunt went off, intentionally, on a side issue.

"I have heard you say 'What the deuce' before now, Boy. But I am glad you appear to realize, judging by your laboured efforts to suppress them, that these expressions shock me."

6

She looked at him, quizzically, through half-closed lids; but the Boy was wholly earnest.

"Well, you see," he said, "I am trying most awfully hard to be, in every respect, just what you would wish the man who loves you should be."

"Oh, you dear boy," said Christobel Charteris, a flood of sudden feeling softening her face; "I must make you understand that I cannot possibly take you seriously. I shall have to tell you a story no one has ever heard before; a tender little story of a long-ago past. I must tell you the story of my Little Boy Blue. Wait here a few moments, while I go indoors and give orders that we are not to be disturbed."

Rising, she passed up the lawn to the little white house. The Boy's eyes followed her, noting with pride and delight the tall athletic figure, fully developed, gracious in its ample lines, yet graceful in the perfect swing of the well-poised walk. During all his college years he had known that walk; admired that stately figure. He had been in the set which called her "Juno" and "The Goddess"; which crowded to the clubs if there was a chance of watching her play tennis. And now, during two wonderful weeks, he had been admitted, a welcomed guest, to this little old-world oasis, bounded by high red-brick walls, where she dwelt and ruled. Quiet, sunny, happy hours he had spent in the hush of the old garden, strolling up and down the long narrow velvet turf, beneath the spreading trees, from the green postern gate in the right-hand corner of the bottom wall, to the flight of stone steps leading up to the garden-door of the little white house.

The Boy knew, by now, exactly what he wanted. He wanted to marry Christobel Charteris.

7

He must have been rather a brave boy. He looked very youthful and slim as he lay back in his chair, watching the stately proportions of the woman on whom he had set his young heart; very slight and boyish, in his silver-grey suit, with lavender tie, and buttonhole of violas. The Boy was very particular about his ties and buttonholes. They always matched. This afternoon, for the first time, he had arrived without a buttonhole. In the surprise and pleasure of his unexpected appearance, the Aunt had moved quickly down the sunlit lawn to meet and greet him.

Mollie had departed, early that morning. Her final words at the railway station, as her impish little face smiled farewell from the window of her compartment, had been: "Mind, Auntie dear, no mistake about Guy Chelsea! He's a charming fellow; and thank you ever so much for giving me such a good time with him. But you can report to Papa, that Guy Chelsea, and his beautiful properties, and his prospective peerage, and his fifty thousand a year, and his motor-cars, and his flying-machines, are absolutely powerless to tempt me away from my allegiance to Phil. Beside, it so happens, Guy himself is altogether in love with SOME ONE ELSE."

The train having begun to move at the words "You can report to Papa," Mollie finished the remainder of the sentence in a screaming crescendo, holding on to her hat with one hand, and waving a tiny lace pocket-handkerchief, emphatically, with the other. Even then, the Aunt lost most of the sentence, and disbelieved the rest. The atmosphere of love had been so unmistakable during those two weeks; the superabundant overflow had even reached herself more than once, with an almost startling thrill of emotion.

The Boy had been so full of vivid, glowing joie-de-vivre, radiating fun and gaiety around him.

In their sets of tennis, played on her own court across the lane at the bottom of the garden, when she could beat him easily were he handicapped by partnership with Mollie; but in genuine singles, when Mollie had tactfully collapsed on to a seat and declared herself exhausted, his swift agility counterbalanced her magnificent service, and they were so evenly matched that each game proved a keen delight— —

In the quiet teas beneath the mulberry tree, where the incomprehensible atmosphere of unspoken tenderness gilded the light words and laughter, as sunlight touches leaf and flower to gold— —

At the cosy dinners, to which they sometimes asked him, sitting in the garden afterwards in the moonlight; when he would tell them thrilling tales of aviation, describing his initial flights, hairbreadth escapes; the joys of rapid soaring; the dangers of cross-currents, broken propellers, or twisted steering-gear— —

On all these occasions, the Boy—with his enthusiasm, his fun, and his fire—had been the life of the happy trio.

During those evenings, in the moonlight, when he started off on airships, one heart stood still very often while the Boy talked; but it stood still, silently. It was Mollie who clasped her hands and implored him never to fly again; then, in the next breath, begged him to take her as a passenger, on the first possible occasion.

Happy days! But Mollie was the attraction; therefore, with Mollie's departure, they would naturally come to an end.

The Boy had not asked if he might come again; and, for the moment, she forgot that the Boy rarely asked for what he wanted. He usually took it.

9

She had a lonely luncheon; spent the afternoon over letters and accounts, picking up the dull threads of things laid aside during the gay holiday time.

It was not the Professor's day for calling. She was alone until four. Then she went out and sat under the mulberry. The garden was very quiet. The birds' hour of silence was barely over.

Jenkins, the butler, had been sent into the town, so Martha brought out tea; as ample, as carefully arranged, as ever; and—cups for two!

"Why two cups, Martha?" queried Miss Charteris, languidly.

"Maybe there'll be a visitor," said Martha in grim prophetic tones. Then her hard old face relaxed and creased into an unaccustomed smile. "Maybe there is a visitor," she added, softly; for at that moment the postern gate banged, and they saw the Boy coming up the garden, in a shaft of sunlight.

The Aunt walked quickly to meet him. His arrival was so unexpected; and she had been so lonely, and so dull.

"How nice of you," she said; "with the Attraction gone. But Martha seems to have had a premonition of your coming. She has just brought out tea, most suggestively arranged for two. How festive you are, Boy! Why this wedding attire? Are you coming from, or going to, a function? No? Then don't you want tennis after tea—a few good hard sets; just we two, unhandicapped by our dear little Mollie?"

"No," said the Boy; "talk, please, to-day; just we two, unhandicapped by our dear little Mollie. Talk please; not tennis."

He paused beside the border, full of mauve and purple flowers.

"How jolly those little what-d'-you-call-'ems look, in the sunshine," he said.

Then the Aunt noticed that he wore no buttonhole, and that his tie was lavender. She picked four of her little violas, and pinned them into his coat.

"Boy dear," she said, "you are a dandy in the matter of ties and buttonholes; only it is so essentially you, that one rather enjoys it. But this is the first day I have known you to arrive without one, and have need to fall back upon my garden."

"It is a first day," said the Boy, dropping into step with her, as she moved toward the mulberry tree. "It starts a new régime, in the matter of buttonholes, and—other things. I am going to have seven days, and this is the first."

"Really?" smiled the Aunt, amused at the Boy's intense seriousness. "I am flattered that you should spend a portion of 'the first day' with me. Let us have tea, and then you shall tell me why seven days; and where you mean to pass them."

The Boy was rather silent during tea. The Aunt, trying to read his mind, thought at first that he regretted his flannels, and the chance of tennis; then that he was missing Mollie. Whereupon the Aunt repeated her remark that it was nice of him to come, now the Attraction was no longer there.

This gave him the cue for which he waited. His cup was empty, and safely on the grass. The floodgates of the Boy's pent-up love and longing burst open; the unforgettable words, "It was always you I wanted," were spoken; and now he waited for her, under the mulberry tree. She had something to tell him; but, whatever it might be, it could not seriously affect the situation. He had told

11

her—that was the great essential. He would win her in seven days. Already she knew just what he wanted—a big step for the first day. He looked up, and saw her coming.

She had regained her usual calm. Her eyes were very kind. She smiled at the Boy, gently.

She took her seat in a low basket-work chair. He had leapt to his feet. She motioned him to another, just opposite hers. She was feeling rather queenly. Unconsciously her manner became somewhat regal. The Boy enjoyed it. He knew he was bent upon winning a queen among women.

"I am going to tell you a story," she said.

"Yes?" said the Boy.

"It is about my Little Boy Blue."

"Yes?"

"You were my Little Boy Blue."

"I?"

"Yes; twenty years ago."

"Then I was six," said the Boy, quite unperturbed.

"We were staying at Dovercourt, on the east coast. Our respective families had known each other. I used to watch you playing on the shore. You were a very tiny little boy."

"I dare say I was quite a nice little boy," said the Boy, complacently.

"Indeed you were; quite sweet. You wore white flannel knickers, and a little blue coat."

12

"I dare say it was quite a nice little coat," said the Boy, "and I hope my womenfolk had the tact to call it a 'blazer.'"

"It was a dear little coat—I should say 'blazer,'" said the Aunt; "and I called you my 'Little Boy Blue.' You also had a blue flannel cap, which you wore stuck on the back of your curls. I spoke to you twice, Little Boy Blue."

"Did you?" he said, and his brown eyes were tender. "Then no wonder I feel I have loved you all my life."

"Ah, but wait until you hear my story! The first time I spoke to you, it happened thus. Your nurse sat high up on the beach, in the long line of nurses, gossiping and doing needlework. You took your little spade and bucket, and marched away, all by yourself, to a breakwater; and there you built a splendid sand castle. I sat on the breakwater, higher up, and watched you. You took immense pains; you overcame stupendous difficulties; and every time your little cap fell off, you picked it up, dusted off the sand with the sleeve of your little blue coat, and stuck it on the back of your curly head again. You were very sweet, Little Boy Blue. I can see you now."

The Aunt paused, and let her eyes dwell upon the Boy in appreciative retrospection. If he felt this something of an ordeal, he certainly showed no signs of it. Not for a moment did his face lose its expression of delighted interest.

"Presently," continued the Aunt, "your castle and courtyard finished, you made a little cannon in the centre of the courtyard, for defence. Then you looked around for a cannon-ball. This was evidently a weighty matter, and indeed it turned out to be such. You stood your spade against the breakwater; placed your bucket beside it; readjusted your little cap, and trotted off almost to the

13

water's edge. Your conception of the size of your castle and cannon must have become magnified with every step of those small sturdy feet, for, arrived at the water, you found a huge round stone nearly as large as your own little head. This satisfied you completely, but you soon found you could not carry it in your hands. You spent a moment in anxious consideration. Then you took off your little blue coat, spread it upon the sand, rolled the cannon-ball upon it, tied the sleeves around it, picked up the hem and the collar, hoisted the heavy stone, and proceeded slowly and with difficulty up the shore. Every moment it seemed as if the stone must fall, and crush the bare toes of my Little Boy Blue. So I flew to the rescue.

"'Little Boy Blue,' I said, 'may I help you to carry your stone?'

"You paused, and looked up at me. I doubt if you had breath to answer while you were walking. Your little face was flushed and damp with exertion; the blue cap was almost off; you had sand on your eyebrows, and sand on your little straight nose. But you looked at me with an expression of indomitable courage and pride, and you said: 'Fanks; but I always does my own cawwying.' With that you started on, and I fell behind—rebuffed!"

"Surly little beast!" ejaculated the Boy.

"Not at all," said the Aunt. "I won't have my Little Boy Blue called names! He showed a fine independence of spirit. Now hear what happened next.

"Little Boy Blue had almost reached his castle, with his somewhat large, but otherwise suitable, cannon-ball, when his nurse, glancing up from her needlework, perceived him staggering along in his shirt-sleeves, and also saw the use to which he was putting his flannel coat. She threw aside the blue over-all she was making,

14

rushed down the shore, calling my Little Boy Blue every uncomplimentary compound noun and adjective which entered her irate and flurried mind; seized the precious stone, unwound the little jacket, flung the stone away, shook out the sand and seaweed, and straightened the twisted sleeves. Then she proceeded to shake the breath out of my Little Boy Blue's already rather breathless little body; put on the coat, jerked him up the shore, and plumped him down with his back to the sea and his castle, to sit in disgrace and listen, while she told the assembled nurses what a 'born himp of hevil' he was! I could have slain that woman! And I knew my little Boy Blue had no dear mother of his own. I wanted to take him in my arms, smooth his tumbled curls, and comfort him. And all this time he had not uttered a sound. He had just explained to me that he always did his own carrying, and evidently he had learned to bear his childish sorrows in silence. I watched the little disconsolate blue back, usually so gaily erect, now round with shame and woe. Then I bethought me of something I could do. I made quite sure he was not peeping round. Then I went and found the chosen stone, and it was heavy indeed! I carried it to the breakwater, and deposited it carefully within the courtyard of the castle. Then I sat down behind the breakwater, on the other side, and waited. I felt sure Little Boy Blue would come back for his spade and bucket.

"Presently the nurses grew tired of bullying him. The strength of his quiet non-resistance proved greater than their superior numbers and brute force. Also his intelligent little presence was, undoubtedly, a check upon their gossip. So he was told he might go; I conclude, on the understanding that he should 'be a good boy' and carry no more 'nasty heavy stones.' I saw him rise and shake the dust of the nurses' circle off his little feet! Then he pushed back his curls, and, without looking to the right or to the left, trotted straight to his castle. I wondered he did not glance, however

15

hopelessly, in the supposed direction of the desired stone. But, no! He came gaily on; and the light of a great expectation shone in his brown eyes.

"When he reached the breakwater, and found his castle, there—safely in the courtyard—reposed the mighty cannon-ball. He stood still a moment, looking at it; and his cheeks went very pink. Then he pulled off his little cap, and turned his radiant face up to the blue sky, flecked with fleeting white clouds. And—'Fank de Lord,' said my Little Boy Blue."

There were unconcealed tears in the Aunt's kind eyes, and she controlled her quiet voice with difficulty. But the glory of a great gladness had come over the Boy. Without as yet explaining itself in words, it rang in his voice and laughter.

"I remember," he said. "Why, of course I remember! Not you, worse luck; but being lugged up the shore, and fearing I had lost my cannon-ball. And, you know, as quite a tiny chap, I had formed a habit of praying about all my little wants and woes. I sometimes think, how amused the angels must have been when my small petitions arrived. There was a scarecrow, in a field, I prayed for, regularly, every night, for weeks. I had been struck by the fact that it looked lonely. Then I seriously upset the theology of the nursery, by passing through a course of persistent and fervent prayer for Satan. It appeared as an obvious logical conclusion to my infant mind: that if the person who—according to nurse—spent all his time in going about making everybody naughty, could himself become good, all naughtiness would cease. Also, that anybody must be considered as 'past praying for,' was an idea which nearly broke my small heart With rage and misery, when it was first crudely forced upon me. I think the arch-fiend must have turned away, silent and nonplussed, if he ever chanced to pass by, while a

16

very tiny boy was kneeling up in his crib, pleading with tearful earnestness: 'Please God, bless poor old Satan; make him good an' happy; an' take him back to heaven.' But it used to annoy nurse considerably, when she came into the same prayer, with barely a comma between."

"Oh, my Little Boy Blue!" cried the Aunt. "Why was I not your mother!"

"Thank goodness, you were not!" said the Boy, imperturbably. "I don't want you for a mother, dear. I want you for my wife."

"So you had prayed about the stone?" remarked the Aunt, hurriedly.

"Yes. While seated there in disgrace, I said: 'Please God, let an angel find my cannon-ball, which howwid old nurse fwowed away. An' let the angel cawwy it safe to the courtyard of my castle.' And I was not at all surprised to find it there; merely very glad. So you see, Christobel, you were my guardian angel twenty years ago. No wonder I feel I have known and loved you, all my life."

"Wait until you hear the rest of my story, Little Boy Blue. But I can testify that you were not surprised. Your brown eyes were simply shining with faith and expectation, as you trotted down the shore. But—who said you might call me 'Christobel'?"

"No one," replied the Boy. "I thought of it myself. It seemed so perfect to be able to say it on the first of my seven days. And, if you consider, I have never called you 'Miss Charteris.' You always seemed to me much too splendid to be 'Miss' anything. One might as well say 'Miss Joan of Arc' or 'Miss Diana of the Ephesians.' But of course I won't call you 'Christobel' if you would rather not."

17

"You quite absurd boy!" said the Aunt, laughing. "Call me anything you like—just for your seven days. But you have not yet told me the meaning or significance of these seven days."

The Boy sat forward, eagerly.

"It's like this," he said. "I have always loved the story of how the army of Israel marched round Jericho during seven days. It appeals to me. The well-garrisoned, invincible city, with its high walls and barred gates. The silent, determined army, marching round it, once every day. Apparently nothing was happening; but, in reality, their faith, enthusiasm, and will-power were undermining those mighty walls. And on the seventh day, when they marched round seven times to the blast of the priestly trumpets; at the seventh time, the ordeal of silence was over; leave was given to the great silent host to shout. So the rams' horns sounded a louder blast than ever; and then, with all the pent-up enthusiasm born of those seven days of silent marching, the people shouted! Down fell the walls of Jericho, and up the conquerors went, right into the heart of the citadel.... I am prepared to march round in silence, during seven days; but on the seventh day, Jericho will be taken."

"I being Jericho, I conclude," remarked the Aunt, dryly. "I cannot say I have particularly noticed the silence. But that part of the programme would be decidedly dull; so we will omit it, and say, from the first: 'little Boy Blue, come blow me your horn!'"

"I shall blow it all right, on the seventh day," said the Boy, "and when I do, you will hear it."

He got up, came across, and knelt by the arm of her chair.

"I shall walk right up into the heart of the citadel," he said, "when the gates fly open, and the walls fall down; and there I shall find you, my Queen; and together we shall 'inherit the kingdom.' O dear unconquered Citadel! O beautiful, golden kingdom! Don't you wish it was the seventh day now, Christobel?"

His mouth looked so sweet, as he bent over her and said "Christobel," with a queer little accent on the final syllable, that the Aunt felt momentarily dizzy.

"Go back to your chair, at once, Boy," she whispered.

And he went.

Neither spoke a word, for some minutes. The Boy lay back, watching the mysterious moving of the mulberry leaves. The triumphant happiness in his face was a rather breathless thing to see. It made you want to hear a great orchestra burst into the Hallelujah Chorus.

The Aunt watched the Boy, and wondered whether she must tell him about the Professor, before the seventh day; and what he would say, when she did tell him; and how Jericho would feel when the army of Israel, with silent trumpets and banners drooping, marched disconsolate away, leaving its walls still standing; its gates still barred. Poor walls, supposed to be so mighty! Already they were trembling. If the Boy had not been so chivalrously obedient, he could have broken into the citadel, five minutes ago. Did he know? .... She looked at his radiant face.... Yes; he knew. There were not many things the Boy did not know. She must not allow the seven days, even though she could absolutely trust his obedience and his chivalry. She must tell him the rest of the story, and send him away to-day. Poor invading army, shorn of its glad triumph! Poor Jericho, left desolate! It was decidedly unusual to be compared to Jericho, and Diana of the Ephesians, and

19

Joan of Arc, all in the same conversation; and it was rather funny to enjoy it. But then most things which happened by reason of the Boy were funny and unusual. He would always come marching 'as an army with banners.' The Professor would drive up to Jericho in a fly, and knock a decorous rat-tat on the gate. Would the walls tremble at that knock? Alas, alas! They had never trembled yet. Would they ever tremble again, save for the march-past of the Boy? Would the gates ever really fly open, except to the horn-blast of little Boy Blue? ... The Aunt dared not think any longer. She felt she must take refuge in immediate action.

"Boy dear," she said, in her most maternal voice, "come down from the clouds, and listen to me. I want to tell you the rest of the story of my Little Boy Blue."

He sprang up, and came and sat on the grass at her feet. All the Boy's movements were so bewilderingly sudden. They were over and done, before you had time to consider whether or no you intended to allow them. But this new move was quite satisfactory. He looked less big and manly, down on the grass; and she really felt maternal, with his curly head so close to her knee. She even ventured to put out a cool motherly hand and smooth the hair back from his forehead, as she began to speak. She had intended to touch it only once—just to accentuate the fact of her motherliness—but it was the sort of soft thick hair which seemed meant for the gentle passing through it of a woman's fingers. And the Boy seemed to like it, for he gave one long sigh of content, and leaned his head against her knee.

"Now I must tell you," said the Aunt, "of the only other time when I ventured to speak to my Little Boy Blue. He had come to his favourite place beside the breakwater. The tide had long ago swept away castle, courtyard, and cannon; but the cannon-ball was still there. It partook of the nature of 'things that remain.' Heavy stones usually do! When I peeped over the breakwater, Little Boy Blue was sitting on the sand. His sturdy legs were spread wide. His bare toes looked like ten little pink sea-shells. Between his small brown knees, he had planted his bucket. His right hand wielded a wooden spade, on the handle of which was writ large, in blue pencil: Master Guy Chelsea. He was bent upon filling his bucket with sand. But the spade being long, and the bucket too close to him—(Boy, leave my shoe alone! It does not require attention)—most of the sand missed the bucket, and went over himself. I heard him sigh rather wearily, and say 'Blow!' in a tired little voice. I leaned over the breakwater. 'Little Boy Blue,' I said, 'may I play with you, and help you to fill your bucket with sand?'

"Little Boy Blue looked up. His curls, his eyebrows, his long dark eyelashes were full of sand. There was sand on his little straight nose. But no amount of sand could detract from the dignity of his little face, or weaken its stern decision. He laid down his spade, put up a damp little hand, and, lifting his blue cap to me, said: 'Fanks; but I don't like girls.' Oh, Master Guy Chelsea, how you snubbed me!"

The Boy's broad shoulders shook with laughter, but he captured the hand still smoothing his hair; and, drawing it down to his lips, kissed it gently, back and palm, and then each finger.

"Poor kind-hearted, well-meaning little girl," he said. "But she must admit, little girls of seven are not always attractive to small boys of six."

"I was not seven," said the Aunt, with portentous emphasis. "Leave go of my hand, Boy, and listen. When you were six, I was sixteen."

21

This bomb of the Aunt's was received with a moment's respectful silence, as befitted the discharge of her principal field-piece. Then the Boy's gay voice said:

"And what of that, dear? When I was six, you were sixteen. When I was twenty, you were twenty-nine——"

"Thirty, Boy; thirty! Be accurate. And now—you are twenty-six, and I am getting on towards forty——"

"Thirty-six, dear, thirty-six! Be accurate!" pleaded the Boy.

"And when you are forty, I shall be fifty; and when you are fifty, Boy—only fifty; a man is in his prime at fifty—I shall be sixty."

"And when I am eighty," said the Boy, "you will be ninety—an old lady is in her prime at ninety. What a charming old couple we shall be! I wonder if we shall still play tennis. I think quite the jolliest thing to do, when we are very very old—quite decrepit, you know—will be to stay at Folkestone, and hire two bath-chairs, with nice active old men to draw them; ancient, of course, but they would seem young compared to us; and then make them race on the Leas, a five-pound note to the winner, to insure them really galloping. We would start at the most crowded time, when the band was playing, and race in and out among lots of other bath-chairs going slowly, and simply terrified at us. Let's be sure and remember to do it, Christobel, sixty years from to-day. Have you a pocket-book? I shall be a gay young person of eighty-six, and you-"

"Boy dear," she said, bending over him, with a catch in her voice; "you must be serious and listen. When I have said that which I must say, you will understand directly that it is no use having your seven days. It will be better and wiser to raise the siege at once, and march away. Listen! ... Hush, stay perfectly still. No; I can say what

22

I am going to say more easily if you don't look at me.... Please, Boy; please.... I told you my 'Little Boy Blue stories' to make you realize how very much older I am than you. I was practically grown up, when you were still a dear delightful baby. I could have picked you up in my arms and carried you about. Oh, cannot you see that, however much I loved him—perhaps I should rather say: just because I love him, because I have always wanted to help him carry his heavy stones; make the best of his life, and accomplish manfully the tasks he sets himself to do—I could not possibly marry my Little Boy Blue? I could not, oh I could not, let him tie his youth and brightness to a woman, staid and middle-aged, who might almost be his mother!"

The earnest, anxious voice, eager in its determined insistence, ceased.

The Boy sat very still, his head bent forward, his brown hands clasping his knees. Then suddenly he knelt up beside her, leaned over the arm of her chair, and looked into her eyes. There was in his face such a tender reverence of adoration, that the Aunt knew she need not be afraid to have him so near. This was holy ground. She put from off her feet the shoes of doubt and distrust; waiting, in perfect calmness, to hear what he had to say.

"Dear," murmured the Boy, tenderly, "your little stories might possibly have had the effect you intended—specially the place where you paused and gazed at me as if you saw me still with sand upon my nose, and ten pink toes like sea-shells! That was calculated to make any chap feel youngish, and a bit shy. Wasn't it? Yes; they might have told the way you meant, were it not for one dear sentence which overshadows all the rest. You said just now: 'I knew my little Boy Blue had no mother. I wanted to take him in my arms, smooth his curls, and comfort him.' Christobel, that dear wish of

23

yours was a gift you then gave to your Little Boy Blue. You can't take it away now, because he has grown bigger. He still has no mother, no sisters, no near relations in the world. That all holds good. Can you refuse him the haven, the help, the comfort you would have given him then, now — when at last he is old enough to know and understand; to turn to them, in grateful worship and wonder? Would you have me marry a girl as feather-brained, as harum-scarum, as silly as I often am myself? You suggest Mollie; but the Boy Blue of to-day agrees with his small wise self of twenty years ago and says: 'Fanks, but I don't like girls!' Oh, Christobel, I want a woman's love, a woman's arms, a woman's understanding tenderness! You said, just now, you wished you had been my mother. Does not the love of the sort of wife a fellow really wants, have a lot of the mother in it too? I've been filled with such a glory, Christobel, since you admitted what you felt for your Little Boy Blue because I seemed to know, somehow, that having once felt it, though the feeling may have gone to sleep, you could never put it quite away. But, if your Little Boy Blue came back, from the other end of the world, and wanted you— —"

The Boy stopped suddenly, struck dumb by the look on the beautiful face beneath his. He saw it pale to absolute whiteness, while the dear firm lips faltered and trembled. He saw the startled pain leap into the eyes. He did not understand the cause of her emotion, or know that he had wakened in that strongly repressed nature the desperate hunger for motherhood, possible only to woman at the finest and best.

She realized now why she had never forgotten her Little Boy Blue of the Dovercourt sands. He, in his baby beauty and sweetness, had wakened the embryo mother in the warm-hearted girl of sixteen. And now he had come back, in the full strength of his young

24

manhood, overflowing with passionate ideality and romance, to teach the lonely woman of thirty-six the true sweet meaning of love and of wifehood.

Her heart seemed to turn to marble and cease beating. She felt helpless in her pain. Only the touch of her Little Boy Blue, or of baby Boy Blues so like him, that they must have come trotting down the sands of life straight from the heaven of his love and hers, could ever still this ache at her bosom.

She looked helplessly up into his longing, glowing, boyish face—so sweet, so young, so beautiful.

Should she put up her arms and draw it to her breast?

She had given no actual promise to the Professor. She had not mentioned him to the Boy.

Ah, dear God! If one had waited twelve long years for a thing which was to prove but an empty husk after all! In order not to fail the possible expectations of another, had she any right to lay such a heavy burden of disappointment upon her little Boy Blue? And, if she must do so, how could she best help him to bear it?

"Fanks," came a brave little voice, with almost startling distinctness, across the shore of memory; "Fanks, but I always does my own cawwying."

At last she found her voice.

"Boy dear," she said, gently; "please go now. I am tired."

Then she shut her eyes.

In a few seconds she heard the gate close, and knew the garden was empty.

25

Tears slipped from between the closed lids, and coursed slowly down her cheeks. The only right way is apt to be a way of such pain at the moment, that even those souls possessing clearest vision and endowed with strongest faith, are unable to hear the golden clarion-call, sounding amid the din of present conflict: "Through much tribulation, enter into the kingdom."

Thus hopeless tears fell in the old garden.

And Martha, the elderly housekeeper, faithful but curious, let fall the lath of the green Venetian blind covering the storeroom window, through which she had permitted herself to peep. As the postern gate closed on the erect figure of the Boy, she dropped the blind and turned away, an unwonted tear running down the furrows of her hard old face.

"Lord love 'im!" she said. "He'll get what he wants in time. There's not a woman walks this earth as couldn't never refuse 'im nothing."

With which startling array of negatives, old Martha compiled one supreme positive in favour of the Boy, leaving altogether out of account—alas!—the Professor.

Then she wiped her eyes with her apron, and chid her nose harshly for an unexpected display of sentiment.

And the Boy tramped back to his hotel with his soul full of glory, knowing his first march round had been to some purpose. The walls of the belovèd Citadel had trembled indeed.

"And the evening and the morning were the first day."

THE SECOND DAY

MISS CHARTERIS TAKES CONTROL

The Boy arrived in flannels, his racket under his arm. He came in, as usual, through the little green gate in the red-brick fruit-wall at the bottom of the garden. From the first, he had taken this privilege, which as a matter of fact had never been accorded to anybody.

The Professor always entered by the front door, placed his umbrella in the stand, wet or shine; left his goloshes on the mat: hung up his cap and gown, and followed Jenkins into the drawing-room. Though he had called regularly, twice a week, during the last dozen years—first on his old friend and tutor, Professor Charteris; after his death, on his widow and daughter; and, when Miss Charteris was left alone, on herself only—he never failed to knock and ring; nor did he ever enter unannounced.

The Boy had dashed in at the garden gate on the occasion of his second visit, and appeared to consider that he had thus created a precedent which should always be followed.

Once, and once only—on her thirtieth birthday—the Professor had brought Miss Charteris a bouquet; but, being very absent-minded, he deposited the bouquet on the mat, and advanced into the drawing-room carrying his goloshes in his left hand. Having shaken hands with his right, he vaguely presented the goloshes. Miss Charteris, never at a loss where her friends were concerned, took the Professor's goloshes from his hand, carried them out into the hall, found the bouquet on the mat, and saved the situation by

27

putting the flowers in water, and thanking the Professor with somewhat more hilarity than the ordinary presentation of a bouquet would have called forth.

But to return to the second day. The Boy arrived in flannels, and tea was a merry meal. The Boy wanted particulars concerning the marriage, which had taken place a year or so before, between Martha—maid of thirty years' standing, now acting as cook-housekeeper to Miss Charteris—and Jenkins, the butler. The Boy wanted to know which proposed, Jenkins or Martha; in what terms they announced the fact of their engagement, to Miss Charteris; whether Jenkins ever "bucked up and looked like a bridegroom," and whether Martha wore orange-blossom and a wedding veil. He extorted the admission that Christobel had been present at the wedding, and insisted on a detailed account; over which, when given at last, he slapped his knee so often, and went into such peals of laughter, that Miss Charteris glanced anxiously towards the kitchen and pantry windows, which unfortunately looked out on the garden.

The Boy expatiated on his enthusiastic admiration for Martha; but at the same time was jolly well certain he would have bolted when it came to "I, Martha, take thee, Jenkins," had he stood in the latter's shoes. Miss Charteris did not dare admit, that as a matter of fact the sentence had been: "I, Martha, take thee, Noah." That the meek Jenkins should possess so historical and patriarchal a name, would completely have finished the Boy, who was already taking considerable risks by combining much laughter with an unusually large number of explosive buns.

The Boy would have it, that, excepting in the rôle of bride and subsequent conjugal owner and disciplinarian, Martha was perfect.

28

Miss Charteris admitted Martha's unrivalled excellence as a cook, her economy in management, and fidelity of heart. But Martha had a temper. Also, though undoubtedly a superficial fault, yet trying to the artistic eye of Miss Charteris, Martha's hair was apt to be dishevelled and untidy.

"It is a bit wispy," admitted the Boy, reluctantly. "Why don't you tell her so?"

Miss Charteris smiled. "Boy dear, I daren't! It would be as much as my place is worth, to make a personal observation to Martha!"

"I'll tell her for you, if you like," said the Boy, coolly.

"If you do," warned Miss Charteris, "it will be the very last remark you will ever make in Martha's kitchen, Boy."

"Oh, there are ways of telling," said the Boy, airily; and pinched an explosive bun.

After tea they took their rackets and strolled down the lawn, pausing a moment while she chose him a buttonhole. The tie was orange on this second day, and she gathered the opening bud of a William Allen Richardson rose. She smiled into its golden heart as she pinned it in his white flannel coat. Somehow it brought a flash of remembrance of the golden heart of Little Boy Blue, who could not bear that any one should be past praying for, or that even a scarecrow should seem lonely.

They crossed the lane and entered the paddock; tightened the net on the tennis-court; chose out half a dozen brand-new balls, and settled down to fast and furious singles.

Miss Charteris played as well as she had ever played in her life; but the Boy was off his service, and she beat him six to four. Next time,

29

he pulled off 'games all,' but lost the set; then was beaten, three to six.

Miss Charteris was glowing with the exercise, and the consciousness of being in great form.

"Boy dear!" she called, as she played the winning stroke of the third set, "I'm afraid you're lazy to-day!"

The Boy walked up to the net, and looked at her through his racket.

"I'm not lazy," he said; "but I'm on the wrong side of Jordan. This sort of thing is waste of time. I want to go over, and start marching."

"Don't be absurd, Boy. I prefer this side Jordan, thank you; and you shall stay here until you beat me."

The Boy won the next set.

It was deliciously cool and quiet under the mulberry-tree.

The Boy was quite subdued—for him. He seemed inclined to do his marching in silence, on this second day.

Miss Charteris felt her mental balance restored. She held the reins to-day, and began considering how to deal wisely with the Boy. So much depended upon how she managed him.

At length she said: "Boy, when you were at Trinity, I often used to see you. I knew you were my Little Boy Blue of all those years ago. I used to feel inclined to send for you, talk to you for your good, and urge you to set to, and do great things; but I remembered the stone, and the bucket; and I did not want to let myself in for a third snubbing."

The Boy smiled. "Did you think me a lazy beggar?" he asked. "I wasn't really, you know. I did quite a good deal of all kinds of things. But I didn't want to get played out. I wanted to do things all the rest of my life. Fellows who grind at college and come out Senior Wranglers, begin and end there. You don't hear of 'em again."

"I see," said Miss Charteris, amusement in her eyes. "So you felt it wisest to avoid being Senior Wrangler?"

"Just so," said the Boy. "I was content with a fairly respectable B.A. and I hope you saw me take it. How rotten it is, going up in a bunch, all hanging on to an old chap's fingers."

"Boy, Boy! I know all about you! You wasted golden opportunities; you declined to use your excellent abilities; you gave the authorities an anxious time. You were so disgracefully popular, that everybody thought your example the finest thing to follow, and you were more or less responsible for every lark and row which took place during your time."

The Boy did not smile. He looked at her, with a quaint, innocent seriousness, which made her feel almost uncomfortable.

"Dear," he said, "I had plenty of money, and heaps of friends, and I wanted to have a good time. Also I wanted all the other fellows to have a good time; and I enjoyed getting the better of all the old fogies who had forgotten what youth was like—if they'd ever known it. And I had no mother to ask me questions, and no sisters to turn up at my rooms unexpectedly. But I can tell you this, Christobel. I hope to be married soon; and I hope to marry a woman so sweet and noble and pure, that her very presence tests a man's every thought, feeling, and memory. And I can honestly look into your dear eyes and say: My wife will be welcome to know

31

every detail of every prank I ever played in Cambridge; nor is there a thing in those three years I need feel ashamed of her knowing. There! Will that do?"

Miss Charteris threw out a deprecatory hand. "Oh, Boy dear!" she said. "I never doubted that. My Little Boy Blue, don't I know you? But I cannot let you talk as if you owe me any explanations. How curious to think I saw you so often during those years, yet we never actually met."

The Boy smiled. "Yes," he said, "we were all awfully proud of you, you know. What was it you took at Girton?"

Miss Charteris mentioned, modestly, the highest honours in classics as yet taken by a woman. The Boy had often heard it before. But he listened with bated breath.

"Yes," he said, "we were awfully proud of it, because of your tennis, and because of you being—well, just you. If you had been a round-shouldered little person in a placket, we should have taken it differently. We always called you 'The Goddess,' because of your splendid walk. Did you know?"

"No, Boy, I did not know; but I confess to feeling immensely flattered. Only, take a friend's advice, and avoid conversational allusions to plackets, because you are obviously ignorant of the meaning of the word. And now, tell me? Having successfully escaped so serious a drawback to future greatness as becoming Senior Wrangler, on what definite enterprise have you embarked?"

"Flying," said the Boy, sitting forward in his chair. "I am going to break every record. I am going to fly higher, farther, faster, than any man has ever flown before. This week, if I had not stayed on here—you know originally I came up only for the 'May week'—I

32

was to have done a Channel flight. Ah, you don't know what it means, to own three flying-machines, all of different make, and each the best of its kind! You feel you own the world! And then to climb into your seat and go whirling away, with the wonderful hum in your ears, mastering the air—the hitherto invincible air. May I tell you what I am going to do for my next fly? Start from the high ground between Dover and Folkestone; fly over the Channel; circle round Boulogne Cathedral—you remember the high dome, rising out of the old town surrounded by the ramparts? Then back across the Channel, and to ground again at Folkestone; all in one flight; and I hope to do it in record time, if winds are right."

"And if winds are wrong, Boy? If you rush out and take the horrid risks of the cross-currents you told us about? If something happens to your propeller, and you fall headlong into the sea?"

"Oh, it's all U P then," said the Boy, lightly. "But one never expects that sort of thing to happen; and when it does, all is over so quickly that there is no time for anticipation. Beside, there must be pioneers. Every good life given, advances the cause."

Christobel Charteris looked at him. His was not the terrible, unmistakable, relentless face of the bird-man. He was brilliant with enthusiasm, but it was the enthusiasm of the sportsman, keen to excel; of Young England, dauntless, fearless, eager to break records. The spirit of the true bird-man had not, as yet, entered into her Little Boy Blue.

She pressed her hand upon her bosom. It ached still.

"Boy dear," she said, softly. "Has it ever struck you that, if you marry, your wife—whoever she might be—would most probably want you to give up flying? I cannot imagine a woman being able to bear that a man who was her all, should do these things."

33

The Boy never turned a hair! He did not bound in his seat. He did not even look at her.

"Why, of course, dear," he said, "if you wished it, I should give up flying, like a shot, and sell my aeroplanes. I know plenty of chaps who would like to buy them to-morrow. And I'll tell you what we would do. We'd buy the biggest, most powerful motor-car we could get, and we'd tear all over the country, exceeding the speed-limit, and doing everything jolly we could think of. That would be every bit as good as flying, if—if we did it together. I say, Christobel—do you know how to make a sentence of 'together'? Just three words: to get her! That's what 'together' spells for me now."

Miss Charteris smiled. "You might have taken honours in spelling, Boy. And I am not the sort of person who enjoys exceeding speed-limits. Also I am afraid I have a troublesome habit of always wanting to stop and see all there is to see."

But the Boy was infinitely accommodating. "Oh, we wouldn't exceed the speed-limit—much. And we would stop everywhere, and see everything. You should breakfast in London; lunch at the Old White Horse, Mr. Pickwick's inn at Ipswich; have tea at the Maid's Head, beneath the shadow of Norwich Cathedral, where you could wash your hands in Queen Elizabeth's fusty old bedroom—what a lot of bedrooms Queen Elizabeth slept in, and made them all fusty—and have time to show me Little Boy Blue's breakwater at Dovercourt, before dinner. There's nothing like motoring!"

"It sounds interesting, certainly," said Miss Charteris.

"And then," continued the Boy, in a calm business-like voice, "it's less expensive than flying. You run through fifty thousand a year in

34

no time with aeroplanes. And of course we should want to open both my places. I'm awfully glad I didn't let the tenants in the old home renew their lease. As it is, they turn out in three months. Oh, I say, Christobel, I do believe it is a setting worthy of you. Have you ever seen it? The great hall, the old pictures, the oak staircase—I once rode down it on my rocking-horse and came to utter smash. And outside—the park, the lake, the beech avenue, the rose-garden, the peacocks. And a funny little old village belongs to us. Think how the people must want looking after. I believe you would like it all—I really believe you would! And think, ah, just think what it would be to me, to see my own splendid wife, queen over everything in my dear jolly old home! Hullo!—Hark to all the clocks! What is that striking? Seven? Oh, I say! I'm dining with the Master to-night. I must rush off, and change. Though I was such a bad lot, they all seem quite pleased to see me again. Really they do! Have I stayed too long? ... Sure? ... May I come to-morrow? ... You are most awfully good to me. Good-bye."

And the Boy was gone. He had held her hand, in a firm, strong clasp, a second longer than the conventional handshake; his clear eyes, exactly on a level with hers, had looked at her gravely, wistfully, tenderly; and he was gone.

She walked slowly up the lawn. She must write a few letters before post time; then dress for her solitary dinner.

She felt a little flat; quite without cause. What could have been more satisfactory, in every way, than the Boy's visit; in spite of his absurd castles in the air? These must be tactfully demolished to-morrow. To-day, it was wisest just to let him talk.

Poor Little Boy Blue! Instead of the walls of Jericho falling, his own

35

castles in the air would come tumbling about his ears. Poor Little Boy Blue!

She felt she had been completely mistress of the situation to-day, holding it exactly as she wished it to be. There was no need to fear the remaining days.

And when the seven days were over—what then? ... She certainly felt very flat this evening. How suddenly the Boy had gone! There was still so much she wanted to say to him.... And to-morrow was the Professor's afternoon. Mercifully, he never stayed later than four o'clock. It was to be hoped the Boy would not turn up early! But there was never any knowing what the Boy would do.

She smiled as she mounted the flight of stone steps, and passed into the house.

And, outside the postern gate, the Boy threw up his cap, and caught it; then started off and sprinted a hundred yards; then, turning aside, leapt a five-barred gate, and made off across the fields. When he pulled up at last, in his own bedroom, he had just time to tub, shave, and wrestle with his evening clothes. He communed with himself in the few moments of enforced stillness, while he mastered his tie.

"That was all right," he said. "I jolly well worked that all right! There was nothing to frighten her to-day—not a thing. Dear lips! They never trembled once; and no more turning faint. And, my Goody, how she lectured me! I wonder who's been telling her what. I know why she did it too. She wanted to feel quite sure she was bossing the show. And so she was, bless her! But I marched round! Yes, I jolly well marched round.... Oh, I say! Can't you stop where I put you?" This, to his tie.

36

Then, with her golden rose in his button-hole, fastened by the pin from his flannel coat, off went the Boy to dine with the Master of his college.

"And the evening and the morning were the second day."

THE THIRD DAY

THE BOY INVADES THE KITCHEN

The Boy sat on a corner of the kitchen table, swinging a loose leg, and watching Martha make hot buttered-toast.

He had arrived early, and, finding no one in the garden, had entered the house by the garden-door, to pursue investigations upstairs.

On the mat in the hall he saw a pair of goloshes; in the umbrella-stand, a very large, badly-rolled umbrella; hanging on a peg near by, a professor's cap and gown.

The Boy stood stock still in the middle of the little hall, and looked at the goloshes.

Then from the drawing-room, through the closed door, came the voice of Miss Charteris—full, clear, measured, melodious—reading Greek tragedy.

érrois anaidés, én táchei neanía

declaimed Miss Charteris; and the Boy fled.

Arrived in the kitchen, he persuaded Martha that cigarette smoke was fatal to black-beetles. He went about, blowing fragrant clouds into every possible crack and cranny. Martha watched him, out of the corner of her eye, crawling along under the dresser in his immaculate white flannels, and Martha blessed her stars that her kitchen floor was so spotlessly clean. Only this morning she had remarked to Jenkins that he could very well eat his dinner off the boards. Mercifully, Jenkins—tiresome man though he usually was—had not taken this literally; or he might have made the floor less fit for the Boy's perambulations.

Having taken all this trouble in order to establish his unquestioned right to smoke in Martha's kitchen, and to pose as a public benefactor while so doing, the Boy seated himself on the edge of the table, exactly behind Martha; lighted a fresh "Zenith," and prepared to enjoy himself.

Martha glanced nervously at the smoke, issuing from cracks and holes on all sides. It gave her a feeling that the house was on fire. Of course she knew it was not; but to feel the house is on fire, is only one degree less alarming than to know it is. However, beetles are nasty things; and the condescending kindness and regard for Martha's personal comfort, which crawled about after them in white flannels, was gratifying to a degree.

So Martha turned and gave the Boy one of her unusual smiles. He was very intently blowing rings—"bubbles" Martha called them afterwards, when explaining them to Jenkins; but that was Martha's mistake. They were smoke rings. It was one of the Boy's special accomplishments. He was an expert at blowing rings.

Presently:—"Martha, my duck—" he said suddenly.

Martha jumped. "Bless us, Mr. Guy! What a name!"

"What's the matter with it?" inquired the Boy, innocently. "I consider it a very nice name, and scriptural."

"Oh, I didn't mean m' own name," explained Martha, more flushed

39

than the warmth of the fire warranted. "Not but what m' godfathers and godmothers might well 'ave chosen me a better."

"Oh, don't blame them, overmuch, Martha," said the Boy, earnestly. "You see their choice was limited. If you study your catechism you will find that it had to be 'N' or 'M'—'Naomi' or 'Martha.' Even at that early age, they thought you favoured 'Martha' rather than 'Naomi'; so they named you 'Martha.'"

"Well I never!" exclaimed Mrs. Jenkins. "'N' or 'M'! So it is! Now I never noticed that before. We live and learn! And Jenkins—silly man—'as always bin annoyed that they named 'im 'Noah.' But how about when you was christened, Mr. Guy?"

"Oh," explained the Boy, with a wave of his cigarette, "I was christened a bit later than you, Martha; and, by that time, Parliament had sat in solemn convocation, and had brought in a Bill to the effect that all needless and vexatious limitations and restrictions in the Prayer Book might for the future be disregarded. The first to go was 'N' or 'M.'"

"Well, I never!" said Martha. "I wish they'd ha' done it afore my time."

"You see," expounded the Boy, who was enjoying himself vastly, and getting the conjunction of the goloshes and the Greek play off his mind; "you see, Martha, those progressive Bills, intimately affecting the whole community, of vital importance to the nation at large, are always blocked by the House of Lords. If the Commons could have had their own way, you might have been named 'Lucy' or 'Clara.'"

"I don't incline to 'Lucy' or 'Clara,' sir," said Mrs. Jenkins, decidedly; "being, as they always strikes me, sickly story-book sort of names;

40

but I do like justice and a free country! I always have felt doubtful o' them Lords, since I listened to my married niece's husband, a very respectable journeyman tailor but mostly out of work; and if it's their doing that I'm 'Martha,' well, I shall know what to do with Jenkins's vote—that's all!"

The Boy slapped his leg and rocked. "Martha, you ought to be put up to speak at political meetings. That's the whole thing in a nutshell: cause, effect, results, arguments, everything! Oh, my wig!—Yes, they are a lot of old stick-in-the-muds in the Upper House, aren't they?" pursued the Boy—who had had a long line of dignified ancestors in that much abused place; had an uncle there at the present moment, and was more than likely eventually to have to sit there himself—"a rotten lot of old stick-in-the-muds, Martha; but I think they did well by you. I'd give them the benefit of Jenkins's vote. I really would. I am glad they chose 'M,' not 'N.' Naomi was a widow and dismal. She never made the smallest effort to buck up. But Martha was a nice person; a bit flurried perhaps, and hot-tempered; but well up in cooking, and keen on it. I like Martha."

The Boy sat and meditated. Why did she read Greek plays with a person who left goloshes on the mat, and brought out an ancient umbrella with a waist, on an absolutely cloudless day?

"It wasn't m' own name surprised me, Mr. Guy, sir," remarked Martha, coyly; "it was the name you was pleased to hadd."

The Boy pulled himself together. "Eh, what? Oh, 'Martha, my duck'? I see. I hope you don't mind, Martha. It seemed to me rather a suitable and pretty addition to 'Martha.' You see, yours is a name which cannot be shortened when one feels affectionate. 'Sarah' can be 'Sally'; 'Amelia' can be 'Milly'; 'Caroline' can be 'Carrie'; but

41

'Martha' remains 'Martha' however loving people feel. What does Jenkins call you when he feels affectionate?"

Martha snorted. "Jenkins knows 'is place," she said, jerking the round lid off the stove, and putting on the kettle.

"Jenkins is a model," smiled the Boy.

Then Martha looked round, her feminine curiosity, and perhaps a touch of jealousy, getting the better of her respectful discretion. She had seen so much, and heard so little; and she was a very old family servant.

"What do you call her, Mr. Guy?" she asked, in a confidential whisper, with a jerk of the head toward the mulberry-tree.

"Her?" repeated the Boy, surprised. Then his whole tone softened. It was so sweet to speak her name to some one. "I call her 'Christobel,'" he said, gently.

But Martha wanted to know more. Martha was woman enough to desire an unshared possession of her own. She bent over the fire, stirring it through the bars.

"Mr. Guy, sir, I suppose you don't—I suppose you do—that is to say, sir—Do you call her what you've been pleased to call me?"

"Eh, what?" said the Boy, vaguely.

"Oh, I see. 'Christobel, my——' Oh, no, Martha. No, I don't! Not even when I feel most affectionate." Here the Boy was seized with sudden convulsions, slapped his knee noiselessly, and rocked on the kitchen table. He whispered it, in an ecstasy of enjoyment. "'Christobel, my duck!' Oh, lor! 'Christobel, my duck!' I hope I shall be able to resist telling her. I should have to own I had called Martha so. 'Christobel, my——'"

Martha, wondering at the silence, looked round suddenly. But the Boy had that instant recovered, and was sitting gravely on the corner of the table.

"Martha, my duck," he said, "to return to the original opening of this conversation: has Jenkins ever told you what a nice little wisp of hair you have, behind your left ear?"

"Get along, sir!" retorted Martha, fairly blushing. "You're making game of me."

"Indeed, I'm not," said the Boy, seriously. "If you made it into a curl, Martha, and fastened it with an invisible pin, it would be quite too fascinating. You ask Jenkins. I say, Martha? What's a placket?"

"A placket, sir," said Martha, on her way to fetch something from a shelf near which hung the kitchen mirror; "a placket, sir, is a thing which shows when it shouldn't."

"I see," said the Boy. "Then you couldn't exactly go about in one. Martha, whose goloshes are those, sitting on the mat in the hall?"

Martha snorted. "An old woman's," she said, wrathfully.

The Boy considered this. "And does the umbrella with the waist belong to the same old woman?"

Martha nodded.

"And the Professor's cap and gown, hanging near by?"

Martha hesitated. "'Tain't always petticoats makes an old woman," she said, sententiously.

"Martha, you are pro-foundly right," said the Boy. "Does the Professor stay to tea?"

43

"Thank goodness no, sir. We draw the line at that, 'cept when Miss Hann comes too."

"Who is Miss Hann?"

"She's the Professor's sister." Martha hesitated; poured hot water into the silver teapot; then turned to whisper confidentially, with concentrated dislike: "She's always a-hegging of 'em on!"

"What a curious occupation," remarked the Boy, blowing a smoke-ring. "Does Miss Hann come often?"

"No, Mr. Guy. Thanks be, she's a hinvalid."

"Poor Miss Hann. What's the matter with her?"

Martha snorted. "Fancies herself too much."

"What a curious complaint. What are the symptoms?"

"Fancies herself in a bath-chair," said Martha, scornfully.

"I see," said the Boy. "Oh, poor Miss Hann! I should feel very sick if I fancied myself in a bath-chair. I wish I could meet Miss Hann. I should like to talk to her about the hegging-on business."

"You'd make her sit up," said Martha, with spiteful enjoyment.

"Oh no, I shouldn't," said the Boy. "That would not be kind to an invalid. I should see that she reclined, comfortably; and then I should jolly well flatten her out."

At that moment a shadow fell across the sunny window. Miss Charteris, her guest having departed, passed down the garden steps, and moved across the lawn.

The Boy sprang to his feet. At sight of her, his conscience smote him

44

that he should have thus gossiped and chaffed with old Martha. He suddenly remembered why he had originally found his way to the kitchen.

"Martha," he said; "I want you to let me carry out the tea-tray this afternoon. She doesn't know I am here. She will think it is you or Jenkins, till she looks round. Let me carry it out, Martha, there's a duck!"

"As you please, sir," said Martha; "but if you want her to think it's Jenkins, you must put it down with a clatter. It takes a man to be clumsy."

The Boy walked over to the window. The mulberry-tree was not visible from the kitchen table.

"Don't go there, Mr. Guy!" cried Martha. "Miss Christobel will see you, sir. This window, and the pantry, show from the garden. If you want to 'ave a look at her, go through that door into the storeroom. The Venetian blind is always down in there. There is one crack through which I— —"

Martha stopped short, disconcerted.

"One crack through which you think I could see? Thank you, Martha," said the Boy, readily. "Hurry up with the tray."

He went into the store-room; found Martha's chink, and realized exactly what had been the extent of Martha's view, during the last two days.

Then he bent his hungry young eyes on Christobel.

She was seated in a garden chair, her back to the house, her face towards the postern gate in the old red wall at the bottom of the

45

garden. The rustic table, upon which he would soon deposit the tea-tray, was slightly behind and to the left of her. The sun shone through the mulberry leaves, glinting on the pure whiteness of her gown. She leaned her beautiful head back wearily. Her whole attitude betokened fatigue. He could not see her face; but he felt sure her eyes were open; and he knew her eyes were on the gate.

The Boy's lips moved. "Christobel," he whispered. "Christobel—belovèd?"

She was waiting; and he knew she was waiting for him.

Presently he dropped the lath of the Venetian blind, and turned to go. But first he took out his pocket-book and fastened the lath which lifted most easily, to those above and below it, with halfpenny stamps. He knew old Martha would take a hint from him. There must be no eyes on the mulberry-tree to-day.

In the kitchen the tray was ready; tea freshly made, thin bread-and-butter, cucumber sandwiches; hot buttered-toast in perfection; cornflour buns, warranted to explode; all the things he liked most; and, best of all, cups for two. He grasped the tray firmly with both hands.

"Martha," he said, "you are a jewel! I give you leave to watch me down the lawn from the kitchen window. But when I have safely arrived, turn your attention to your own tea, or I shall look up and shake my fist at your dear nice old face. And, I say, Martha, do you ever write postcards? Because, if you want any ha'penny stamps, you will find some on the storeroom blind. Only, don't want them, Martha, till this week is over, and I am gone."

Whereupon the Boy lifted the tray, and made for the door.

Down the lawn he bore it, and set it safely on the rustic table. He was very deft of movement, was the Boy; yet, remembering his instructions, he contrived to set it down with something of a clatter.

Miss Charteris did not turn her head Her eyes, half closed beneath the long lashes, were on the postern gate.

"Jenkins?" she said.

"Yes, ma'am," replied the Boy, in excellent imitation of the meek tones of Jenkins.

"Should any one call this afternoon, Jenkins, please remember that I am not 'at home.'"

"Hip, hip, hurrah!" said the Boy.

Then she turned—and her face was all, and more than all, he had hoped it might be.

"Oh, Boy," she said. "Oh, Boy dear!"

After that, it was a very happy tea. Neither had been quite natural, nor had they been really true to themselves, the day before; so the delight of meeting seemed to follow a longer parting than the actual twenty-four hours. The Boy's brown eyes rested in tenderness on the hand that filled his cup, and she did not say "Don't"; she merely smiled indulgently, and added the cream and sugar slowly, as if to let him do what he willed.

The hum of bees was in the garden; a sense of youth was in the air. The sunbeams danced among the mulberry leaves.

The Boy insisted upon carrying back the tray, to do away at once with the possibility of interruption from Jenkins. Then he drew their chairs into the deeper shade of the mulberry-tree, a corner invisible from all windows. The Boy had learned a lesson while looking through the storeroom blind.

There they sat and talked, in calm content. It did not seem to matter much of what they spoke, so long as they could lie back facing one another; each listening to the voice which held so much more of meaning in it than the mere words it uttered; each looking into the eyes which had now become clear windows through which shone the soul.

Suddenly the Boy said: "How silly we were, the other day, to talk of the relative ages of our bodies. What do they matter? Our souls are the real you and I. And our souls are always the same age. Some souls are old—old from the first. I have seen an old soul look out of the eyes of a little child; and I have seen a young soul dance in the eyes of an old, old woman. You and I, thank God, have young souls, Christobel, and we shall be eternally young."

He stretched his arms over his head, in utter joyful content with life.

"Go on, Boy dear," said Christobel. "I am not sure that I agree with you; but I like to hear you talk."

"At first," he said, "our bodies are so babyish that our souls do not find them an adequate medium of expression. But by and by our bodies grow and develop; after which come the beautiful years of perfection, ten, twenty, thirty of them, when the young soul goes strong and gay through life, clad in the strong gay young body. Then—gradually, gradually, the strong young soul, in its unwearied, immortal youth, wears out the body. The body grows old, but not the soul. Nothing can age that; and when at last the body quite wears out, the young soul breaks free, and begins again. Youthful souls wear out their bodies quicker than old ones; just as a strong young boy romps through a suit of clothes sooner than a weakly old man. But there is always life more abundant, and a fuller life farther on. So the mating of souls is the all-important thing; and when young souls meet and mate, what does it matter if there be a few years' difference in the ages of their bodies? Their essential youthfulness will surmount all that."

Christobel looked at him, and truly for a moment the young soul in her leapt out to his, in glad response. Then the other side of the question rose before her.

"Ah, but, Boy dear," she said, "the souls express themselves—their needs, their delights, their activities—through the bodies. And suppose one body, in the soul-union, is wearing out sooner than the other; that is hard on the other—hard on both. Boy—my Little Boy Blue—shall I tell you an awful secret? I suppose I sat too closely over my books at Girton; I suppose I was not sufficiently careful about good print, or good light. Anyway—Boy dear—I have to use glasses when I read." She looked wistfully into his bright eyes. "You see? Already I am beginning to grow old." Her sweet lips trembled.

In a moment he was kneeling by the arm of her chair, bending over her, as he did on the first day; but as he did not do yesterday. Suddenly she realized why she had felt so flat yesterday, after he was gone.

He lifted her hand and kissed it gently, back and palm. Then he parted the third finger from the rest, with his own brown ones, and held that against his warm young lips.

She drew her hand slowly away; passed it over his hair; then let it fall upon her lap. She could not speak; she could not move; she could not send him away. She wanted him so—her little Boy Blue, of long ago.

"Old, my Belovèd?" he said. "You—old! Never! Always perfect—perfect to me. And why not wear glasses? Heaps of mere kids wear glasses, and wear them all the time. Only—how alarmingly clever you must look in spectacles, Christobel. It would terrify me now; but by and by it will make me feel proud. I think one would expect glasses to go with those awe-inspiring classical honours. With my barely respectable B.A., I daren't lay claim to any outward marks of erudition." Then, as she did not smile, but still gazed up at him, wistfully, his look softened to still deeper tenderness: "Dear eyes," he murmured, "oh dear, dear eyes," and gently laid his lips on each in turn.

"Don't," she said, with a half sob. "Ah, Boy, don't! You know you must not kiss me."

"Kiss you!" he said, still bending over her. "Do you call that kissing?" Then he laughed; and the joyous love in his laughter wrung her heart. "Christobel, on the seventh day, when the gates fly open, and the walls fall down; when the citadel surrenders; when you admit you are my own—then I shall kiss you; then you will know what kissing really means."

He bent above her. His lips were very near to hers. She closed her eyes and waited. Her own lips trembled. She knew how fearfully it tempted the Boy that her lips should tremble because his were near; yet she let them tremble. She forgot to remember the past; she forgot to consider the future. She was conscious of only one thing: that she wanted her Little Boy Blue to teach her what kissing really meant. So she closed her eyes and waited.

She did not hear him go; but presently she knew he was no longer there.

She opened her eyes.

50

The Boy had walked across the lawn, and stood looking into the golden heart of an opening yellow rose. His back appeared very uncompromising; very determined; very erect.

She rose and walked over to him. As she moved forward, with the graceful dignity of motion which was always hers, her mental balance returned.

She slipped her hand beneath his arm. "Come, Boy," she said; "let us walk up and down, and talk. It is enervating to sit too long in the sunshine."

He turned at once, suiting his step to hers, and they paced the lawn in silence.

When they reached the postern gate the Boy stood still. Something in his look suddenly recalled her Little Boy Blue, when the sand on his small nose could not detract from the dignity of his little face, nor weaken its stern decision.

He took both her hands in his, and looked into her eyes.

"Christobel," he said, "I must go. I must go, because I dare not stay. You are so wonderful this afternoon; so dear beyond expression. I know you trust me absolutely; but this is only the third day; and I cannot trust myself, dear. So I'm off!"

He lifted both her hands to his lips.

"May I go, my Queen?" he said.

"Yes, Boy," she answered. "Go."

And he went.

It was hard to hear the thud of the closing door. For some time she stood waiting, just on the inside. She thought he would come back, and she wished him to find her there, the moment he opened the door.

But the Boy—being the Boy—did not come back.

Presently she returned to her chair, in the shade of the mulberry-tree. She lay, with closed eyes, and lived again through the afternoon, from the moment when the Boy had said: "Hip, hip, hurrah!" There came a time when she turned very pale, and her lips trembled, as they had done before.

At length she rose and paced slowly up the lawn. On her face was the quiet calm of an irrevocable decision.

"To-morrow," she said, "I must tell the Boy about the Professor."

In the middle of the night, Martha, being wakeful, became haunted by the remembrance of the smoke, as it had curled from cracks and keyholes in the kitchen. She felt constrained to put on a wonderful pink wrapper, and go creaking slowly down the stairs to make sure the house was not on fire. Martha's wakefulness was partly caused by the unusual fact of a large and hard curl-paper, behind her left ear.

Miss Charteris was also awake. She was not worried by memories of smoke, or visions of fire; and her soft hair was completely innocent of curl-papers. But she was considering how she should tell the boy about the Professor; and that consideration was not conducive to calm slumber. She heard Martha go creaking down the stairs; and, as Martha came creaking up again, she opened her door, and confronted her.

"What are you doing, Martha?" she said.

Martha, intensely conscious of her curl-paper, was about to answer with more than her usual respectful irritability, when the eyes of the two women—mistress and maid—met, in the light of their respective candles, and a sudden sense of fellowship in the cause of their night vigil passed between them.

Martha smiled—a crooked smile, half ashamed to be seen smiling. When she spoke, her aspirates fell away from her more completely than in the daytime.

"'E went crawlin' about the kitchen," she said, in a muffled midnight whisper; "all in 'is white flannels, puffin' smoke in every crack an' 'ole to kill the beetles. So kind 'e meant it; but I couldn't sleep for wonderin' if the place was smokin' still. I 'ad to go down an' see. 'Ow came you to be awake, Miss Christobel?"

"Things he said in the garden, Martha, have given me food for thought. I began thinking them over; and sleep went."

Martha smiled again—and this time the smile came more easily. "'E 'as a way of keepin' one on the go," she said; "but we'd best be gittin' to sleep now, miss. 'E'll be at it again to-morrow, bless 'is 'eart!" And Martha, in her pink wrapper, lumbered upwards.

But the Boy, who had this disturbing effect on the women who loved him, slept soundly himself, one arm flung high above his tumbled head. And if the sweet mother, who perforce had had to let her dying arms slip from about her baby-boy, almost before his little feet could carry him across a room, saw from above the pure radiance on his lips and brow as he slept, she must have turned to the Emerald Throne with glad thanksgiving for the answer vouchsafed to a dead mother's prayers.

"And the evening and the morning were the third day."

THE FOURTH DAY

CHRISTOBEL SIGNS HER NAME

"I am exhausted," said the Boy, reaching out a long arm, and securing his third piece of hot buttered-toast. "I am ruffled. My usual calm mental poise is overthrown—and on the Sabbath, of all days! Every feather I possess has been rubbed up the wrong way." He lay back in the depths of his chair, stretched out his legs, and looked dejectedly at Christobel.

Her quiet smile enveloped him. Her look was as a cool touch on a hot forehead.

"Poor Little Boy Blue! I thought something was wrong. I should feel a keener anxiety, were the hot buttered-toast less obviously consoling."

"I'll jolly well never go again," said the Boy, with indignation. "Not me!"

"Before you were born, Boy; when I went to school," said Miss Charteris, "we were taught to say 'Not I.' And if you were to tell me where you have been, on this Sabbath afternoon, I might be able to give you more intelligent sympathy."

"I've been to a drawing-room meeting," said the Boy, "and I've heard a woman hold forth. For an hour and a quarter, I've sat stuffed up, breathing the atmosphere of other people's go-to-meeting clothes, and heard a good lady go meandering on, while I had no room for my legs."

"I thought you seemed finding them extra long, Boy. Why did you go to a drawing-room meeting?"

"I went," said the Boy, "because the dear old thing in whose house it was held asked me to go. She used to know my mother. When I was at Trinity she looked me up, often invited me to her charming home, gave me excellent little dinners, followed by the kindest, nicest, most nervous little preachments. Don't look amused, dear. I never failed to profit. I respected her for it. She is as good and genuine as they make 'em; and if she had stood up this afternoon, with her friendly smile, and dear shaky old voice, and given us an exposition of the twenty-third Psalm, we should have all come away quite 'good and happy.' Instead of which—oh, my wig!"

The Boy took an explosive bun, and put it whole into his mouth. "The only way to manage them on Sunday," he explained, as soon as speech was possible, "when sweeping is not the right thing. But let us hope Mollie's papa's 'clerical brethren' won't find it out. There would certainly be less conversation and fewer crumbs, but no fun at all."

"I don't think you need be afraid, Boy dear. Even should such a way out of the difficulty occur to them, I am inclined to think they would prefer the explosion, to the whole bun at a mouthful. It has a rather startling effect, you know, until one gets used to seeing it done. I can't quite imagine an archdeacon doing it, while standing on the hearthrug in conversation with my brother. Now tell me what the good lady said, which you found so trying."

"Oh, she meandered on," grumbled the Boy. "She told us all we should have been, if we had not been what we were; and all we might be, if we were not what we are; and all we shall be, when we are not what we are! She implored us to consider, and weigh well,

55

where we should go, if, by a sudden and unexpected dispensation of Providence, we ceased to be where we then were. I jolly well knew the answer to that; for if Providence had suddenly dispensated—which it didn't, for a good three-quarters of an hour—I should have been here, here, HERE, as fast as my best Sunday boots could carry me!" His brown eyes softened. "Ah, think what 'here' means," he said. "Think! 'Here' means You!"

But Miss Charteris did not wish the conversation to become too meltingly personal.

"What else did she say, Boy?"

He consulted the mulberry leaves, then bounded in his chair. "Ha, I have it! I kept this tit-bit for you. She used an astronomical illustration, I haven't the least idea apropos of what, but she told us exactly how many millions of miles the sun is from the earth; and then she smiled upon us blandly, and said: 'Or is it billions?' Think of that! She said: 'Or is it billions?' in exactly the same tone of voice as she might have said of the bonnet she had on: 'I bought it, at a sale, for elevenpence three farthings, or was it a shilling?'"

"Oh, Boy, you really are naughty! I never connected you with personal sarcasm."

"Yes, but that sort of woman shouldn't," complained the Boy. "And with half Cambridge sitting listening. 'Millions, or is it billions?' Oh lor!"

"Poor thing!" remarked Miss Charteris. "She could not have known that she had in the audience a person who had only just avoided the drawback to future enterprise, of being Senior Wrangler. Had she realized that, she would have been more careful with her figures."

"Tease away!" said the Boy. "I don't care, now I am safe here. Only I shan't tell you any more."

"I don't want to hear any more, Boy. I always enjoy appreciations, even of things I do not myself appreciate. But non-appreciations do not appeal to me. If a person has meant to be effective and proved inadequate, or tried to do good and done harm, I would rather not know it, unless I can help to put matters right. Have some more tea, Boy; and then I want to talk to you myself. I have something rather special to tell you."

The Boy stood up and brought his cup to the little table. When she had filled it, he knelt on one knee beside her, his elbow on the arm of her chair, and drank his tea there.

"I am sorry, dear," he said, presently. "I won't do it again. Perhaps I listened wrong, because I was bored at being there at all. I say, Christobel—it has just occurred to me—did you know my mother?"

The old garden was very still. A hush, as of the Paradise of God, seemed suddenly to fall upon it. As the Boy asked his quiet question, a spirit seemed to hover, between them and the green dome of mulberry leaves above them, smoothing the Boy's tumbled hair, and touching the noble brow of the woman the Boy loved; a gentle, watching, thankful spirit—eternally remembering, and tenderly glad to be remembered. For a few moments the silence was a silence which could not be broken. The Boy lifted wondering eyes to the moving leaves. Christobel laid her hand upon his, as it gripped her chair. An unseen voice seemed to whisper to the Boy— not in the stern tones of the Church, but as an eager, anxious, question: "Wilt thou—have—this woman—to be thy wedded wife?" And silently the Boy replied: "Please God, I will"; and, bending, kissed the hand resting on his.

57

The spell lifted. Christobel spoke.

"Yes, Boy dear, I knew her. I have often wondered whether I might tell you. She and my mother were dear friends. I was thirteen when she died. You were three, poor Little Boy Blue! Two things I specially remember about your mother: the peculiar radiance of her face—a light from within, shining out; and the fact that when she was in a room the whole atmosphere seemed rarefied, beautified, uplifted. I think she lived very near heaven, Boy; and, like Enoch, she walked straight in one day, and came back no more. She 'was not'; for God took her."

Another long holy silence. The mulberry leaves were still. Then the Boy said, softly: "Some day, will you tell me heaps more—details—lots of little things about her? No one ever has. But I seem almost to begin to remember her, when you talk of her. Meanwhile, may I show you this?"

He drew from the inner pocket of his coat, a small well-worn pocket-Bible. Opening it at the fly-leaf, he passed it to Miss Charteris.

"It was hers," he said.

She bent over it and read the inscription:

M. A. Chelsea

"Through faith and patience inherit the promises."

Below, in a delicate writing, traced by a hand that trembled:

To my Baby Boy from his Mother

"I have prayed for thee, that thy faith fail not."

58

She looked at it in silence. How much had this book meant during all these years, to the "Baby Boy"? Had the book in his pocket, and the prayers hovering about him, something to do with the fact that he was still—just Little Boy Blue?

The Boy had taken a fountain pen from his pocket, and was shaking it vigorously over the grass.

Now he passed it to her.

"Write your dear name beneath," he said.

Infinitely touched, she made no comment, raised no question. She took the pen, and wrote just "Christobel."

"And the evening and the morning were the fourth day."

THE FIFTH DAY

GUY CHELSEA TAKES CONTROL

"Now, Sir Boy," said Miss Charteris with decision, "this is your fifth day. Our time is nearly over. You have done most of the talking. You have had things entirely your own way. What? ... Oh, well, almost entirely your own way. I have allowed you to play your Old Testament game to your heart's content. With commendable adaptability, I have been Jericho, and you have marched round. I have been Jericho in my own garden, and have refreshed the invading army with hot buttered-toast and explosive buns. Now it is my turn to take the initiative. Jenkins having removed the tea, and it being too hot for tennis, I am going to ask you to sit still, while I explain to you quite clearly why I must send you away at the close of the seventh day."

She tried to hide her extreme trepidation beneath a tone of gay banter. She hoped it did not sound as forced to him as it did to herself. The Boy's clear eyes were fixed upon her. Had he noticed the trembling of her hands, before she steadied them by laying hold of the arms of her chair?

"So now for a serious talk, if you please, Sir Boy."

"Excuse me, dear," said the Boy, "the Israelites were not allowed to parley."

"You need not parley," said Miss Charteris; "you are requested merely to listen. You may smoke if you like. I understand cigarette

60

smoke is fatal to black-beetles. Possibly it has the same effect on garden insects. Russell tells me we are overrun by snails. Smoke, Boy, if you like."

"Dear," said the Boy, his head thrown back, his hands thrust deep into his coat pockets, "I never have the smallest desire to smoke in your presence. I should feel as if I were smoking in church."

"Oh, you dear amazing altogether absurd boy! Don't look at me like that. And don't say such unexpected things, or I shall be unable to parley satisfactorily."

"When I went to school," remarked the Boy, "and you were an engaging little girl in a pigtail, I was taught to say: 'Do not look at me thus'; at least, masters frequently appeared to think it necessary to make that remark to me. I can't imagine why; because they were not specially worth looking at; excepting that a very large person, in a very angry condition, always presented a spectacle of extreme interest to my juvenile mind. It was so fascinating to watch and see what they would do next. They were like those wooden monkeys and bears you buy in Swiss shops, don't you know? You pull a hanging string, and their legs and arms jump about unexpectedly. One always felt a really angry grown-up was a mere puppet. Unseen fingers were pulling the string; and it was funny to watch. There was an exciting element of danger, too; because sometimes a hand jerked up and boxed your ears."

"Little Boy Blue," she said, "it must have been quite impossible ever to be mildly angry with you. Either one would have waxed impotently furious; or one would have wanted to—to hug you!"

The Boy leapt up.

"Sit down," said Miss Charteris, "or I shall send you away. And I do not wish to do that; because I have quite made up my mind to tell you to-day, a thing which I suppose I ought to have told you long ago; and I tried to do so, Boy; but somehow you always made it impossible. I want to—to tell you about—the Professor." She paused.

It was so very difficult. It was like rolling a heavy stone up a steep hill. And the Boy made no attempt to help her. He lay back with an exaggerated display of resignation. He looked at her with sleepy, amused eyes. And he asked no questions. The army of Israel obviously declined to parley.

"I have long felt I ought to tell you about the Professor," continued Miss Charteris.

The Boy sighed. "I think I jolly well know all there is to know about professors," he said.

"Not about this one," explained Miss Charteris. "He is my Professor."

"Oh, if he's your Professor," said the Boy, sitting up, "of course I am interested. But I am not sure that I approve of you having a tame Professor; especially when it arrives in goloshes, and leaves them in the hall."

"I am afraid nobody will ask whether you approve or not, Little Boy Blue. The Professor has been a great friend of mine during nearly twelve years; and I think I am possibly—in fact, very probably—going to marry the Professor."

"Really?" said the Boy. "May I ask when he proposed?"

"He has not proposed, Boy."

The Boy produced his pocket-book, took out a calendar, and studied it attentively.

"Then I'm afraid you will have some time to wait," he said. "It will not be leap year again until 1912."

This sounded impertinent; but the Boy could no more have been guilty of intentional impertinence toward her, than he could have picked her pocket; and Miss Charteris knew it. There was one thing of which those who had dealings with Christobel Charteris could always be sure—absolute justice. She had seen the Boy's face whiten suddenly, to a terrible pallor, beneath his tan. She knew he was making a desperate fight for self-control. How best could she help? Her own part seemed almost more than she could manage.

"Come here, Boy dear," she said, holding out her hand.

He hesitated one instant; then rose unsteadily to his feet, and came—not to his usual place at the side, bending over her; but in front of her, on one knee, silently waiting.

She bent forward. "Take my hand, Boy."

He took it, in a firm unhesitating clasp. They held each other so, in silence. The colour came back into the Boy's face. The dumb horror died out of his eyes. They smiled into hers again.

"Now promise me, Boy dear, that you will let me tell you all; and that you will try not to misunderstand."

"My dearest," said the Boy, "I promise. But I do not need to say I will try not to misunderstand. I could not misunderstand you, if I tried."

"Then go back to your chair, Boy."

He went. His eyes were bright again.

"Boy, please to understand that I am not engaged to the Professor. Of course, had that been the case, I should have told you, long ago. He has never said one word to me of love or marriage. But he has been a great friend—an intimate friend, intellectually; and I have reason to know that he wishes—has wished for years—a good deal more than he has ever expressed to me. He has waited, Boy; and when anybody has waited nearly twelve years, could one fail them?"

"Why, of course!" cried the Boy, eagerly. "If a man could wait twelve years—good heavens, why shouldn't he wait twenty! A man has no business to wait; or to be able to wait; or to keep a woman waiting. Twelve years? Oh, I say! I didn't wait twelve days. Now, did I?"

She smiled. "You break all speed records, Boy, always. But cannot you understand that all men have not fifty thousand a year, and the world at their feet? Had you been penniless, Boy, you—even you—would have had to wait."

"Not a bit!" said the Boy, stoutly. "I would drive a cab, I would sweep a crossing, I would do anything, or be anything; but I wouldn't wait for the woman I loved; nor would I"—his voice dropped almost to a whisper—"keep the woman who loved me, waiting."

"But suppose she had a comfortable little income of her own; and you had less—much less—to offer her? Surely, Boy, proper pride would keep you from asking her to marry you, until your income at least equalled hers?"

"Not a bit!" said the Boy. "That sort of rot isn't proper pride. It's just selfish false pride. However much a woman had, when a man—a man, mind you, not an old woman, or a thing with no pluck or vertebra—when a man gives a woman his whole love, his whole life, the worship of his whole body, heart, and soul, he has given her that which no money could buy; and were she a millionairess she would still be poor if, from false pride, he robbed her of that gift which was his to give her—and perhaps his alone."

"Boy dear," she said, gently; "it sounds very plausible. But it is so easy to be plausible with fifty thousand a year in the background. Let me tell you about the Professor. He has, of course, his fellowship, and is quite comfortably off now, living as a bachelor, in rooms. But he practically supports his unmarried sister, considerably older than himself, who lives in a tiny little villa, and keeps one maid. The Professor could not afford to marry, and set up a larger establishment, on his present income; at least he apparently thinks he could not. And your theory of robbing the woman who—the woman he loves, does not appear to have occurred to him. But, during all these years he has been compiling an Encyclopedia—I don't suppose you know what an Encyclopedia is, Boy."

"Oh, don't I?" said the Boy. "It's a thing you pile up on the floor to stand upon when you want to fix a new pipe-rack."

Miss Charteris ignored this trying definition of an Encyclopedia.

"The Professor is compiling a wonderful book," she said, with dignity; "and, when it is completed and published, he will be in a position to marry."

"Has he told you so?" inquired the Boy.

"No, Boy. He has never mentioned the subject of marriage to me. But he has told his sister; and she has told me."

"Ha!" said the Boy. "Miss Hann, I suppose. I must say, I distrust Miss Hann."

"What do you know of Miss Ann?" inquired Christobel, astonished.

"Only that she's always a-hegging of 'em on," said the Boy, calmly.

The indignant blood rushed into the fair proud face.

"Boy! You've been gossiping with Martha."

"I have, dear; I admit it. You see, I arrived early, on the third day; found the garden empty; went gaily into the house to look for you. Ran up into the hall; when up got a pair of old goloshes—eh, what? Oh, sorry—up got a pair of new goloshes, and hit me in the eye! A professor's cap and gown hung up, as if at home; and while I meditated upon these things, the voice of my Belovèd was uplifted in loud and sonorous Greek, exclaiming: 'Avaunt, rash youth! Thou impudent intruder!' Can you wonder that I avaunted—to Martha?"

"You will please tell me at once all Martha said to you."

"Of course I will, dear. Don't be vexed. I always meant to tell you, some time or other. I asked her whose were the goloshes; the umbrella with the—er—decided figure; the suspended cap and gown. Martha said they were the Professor's. I inquired whether the Professor stayed to tea. You really can't blame me for asking that; because I had gone to the kitchen for the express purpose of carrying out the tea-tray, yours and mine; but not the Professor's. No possible pleasure could have resulted, either to you, or to me, or to the Professor, from my unexpected appearance with the tea-tray, if the Professor had been there. Now could it? I think it would be

66

nice of you, dear, and only fair, if, remembering the peculiar circumstances of that afternoon, you just said: 'No; it couldn't.'

"Well, I asked Martha whether the Professor stayed to tea, and heard that 'Thank goodness, no!' we drew the line at that, except when Miss Hann came too. With the awful possibility of Miss Hann 'coming too,' on one of my priceless days, I naturally desired a little light thrown on Miss Hann. I was considerably relieved to learn that Miss Hann suffers from the peculiar complaint—mental, I gather—of 'fancying herself in a bath-chair.' This might be no hindrance to the 'hegging on' propensities, but it certainly diminished the chances of the 'coming too.' That was all, dear."

"Boy, you ought to have been ashamed of yourself!"

"So I was, the moment I saw you walk down the lawn. But you really needn't look so indignant. I was working for you, at the same time."

"Working for me?"

"Yes, dear. I told Martha her wisps would look nicer if she curled them. I also suggested 'invisible pins.' If you like I will tell you how I came to know about 'invisible pins'; but it is a very long story, and not specially interesting, for the lady in the case was my great-aunt."

"Oh, Boy," said Miss Charteris, laughing in spite of herself; "I wish you were the size of my Little Boy Blue on the sands at Dovercourt. I would dearly like to shake you."

"Well," he said, "you did more than shake me, just now. You gave me about the worst five minutes I ever had in my life. Christobel? You don't really care about the Professor?"

67

"Boy, dear, I really do. I have cared about him very much, for years."

"Yes, as a woman loves a book; but not as a woman loves a man."

"Explain your meaning, please."

"Oh, hang it all!" exclaimed the Boy, violently. "Do you love his mouth, his eyes, his hair— —?" The Boy choked, and stopped short.

Miss Charteris considered, and replied with careful deliberation. "I do not know that I have ever seen his mouth; he wears a beard. His eyes are not strong, but they look very kind through his glasses. His hair? Well, really, he has not much to speak of. But all these things matter very little. His mind is great and beautiful; his thoughts appeal to me. I understand his way of viewing things: he understands mine. It would be a wonderful privilege to be able to make life easy and happy for one for whom I have so profound a respect and esteem. I have looked upon it, during the last few years, as a privilege which is, eventually, to be mine."

"Christobel," cried the Boy, "it is wrong, it is terrible! It is not the highest. I can't stand it, and I won't. I will not let you give yourself to a wizened old bookworm— —"

"Be quiet, Boy," she said, sharply. "Do you wish to make me really angry? The Professor is not old. He is only fourteen years my senior. To your extreme youth, fifty may seem old. The Professor is in his prime. I am afraid we have nothing to gain, Boy, by prolonging this discussion."

"But we can't leave it at this," said the Boy, desperately. "Where do I come in?"

"My Little Boy Blue, I am afraid you don't come in at all, excepting as a very sweet idyll which, all through the years to come, I shall never forget. You begged for your seven days, and I gave them. But I never led you to assume I could say 'Yes.' Now listen, Boy, and I will tell you the honest truth. I do not know that I am ever going to marry the Professor. I only feel pledged to him from the vague belief that we each consider the other is waiting. Don't break your heart over it, Boy; because it is more than likely it will never come to pass. But—even were there no Professor—oh, Boy dear, I could not marry you. I love my Little Boy Blue more tenderly and deeply than I have ever before loved anything or any one on this earth. But I could not marry a boy, however dearly I loved him; however sweet was his love to me. I am a woman grown, and I could surrender myself wholly, only to a man who would wholly be my mate and master. I cannot pretend to call my Little Boy Blue 'the man I love,' because he is really dearest to me when I think of him, with expectation in his baby-eyes, trotting down the sands to find his cannon-ball.... Oh, Boy, I am hurting you! I hate to hurt you, Boy. Your love is so beautiful. Nothing as perfect will ever touch my life again. Yet I cannot, honestly, give what you ask.... Boy dear, ought I to have told you, quite plainly, sooner? If so, you must forgive me."

The Boy had risen, and stood before her. "You always do the right thing," he said, "and never, under any circumstances, could there be anything for me to forgive you. I have been an egregious young ass. I have taken things for granted, all along the line. What must you think of me! Why should you care? You, with your intellectual attainments, your honours, your high standing in the world of books? Why should you care, Christobel? Why should you care?"

He stood before her, straight and tall and desperately implacable. The exuberant youth had died out of his face. For the first time, she could not see in him her Little Boy Blue.

69

"Why should you care?" he said again.

She rose and faced him. "But I do care, Boy," she said. "How dare you pretend to think I don't? I care very tenderly and deeply."

"Pooh!" said the Boy. "Do you suppose I wished you to marry a bare-toed baby, with sand on its nose?" He laughed wildly; paused and looked at her, then laughed again. "A silly little ass that said it didn't like girls? Oh, I say! I think it's about time I was off. Will you walk down to the gate? ... Thanks. You are always most awfully good to me. I say, Miss Charteris, may I ask the Professor's name?"

"Harvey," she said, quietly. "Kenrick Harvey." The dull anguish at her heart seemed almost more than she could bear. Yet what could she say or do? He was merely accepting her own decision.

"Harvey?" he said. "Why of course I know him. He's not much to look at, is he? But we always thought him an awfully good sort, and kind as they make 'em. We considered him a confirmed bachelor; but—well, we didn't know he was waiting."

They had reached the postern gate. Oh, would he see the growing pain in her eyes? What was she losing? What had she lost? Why did her whole life seem passing out through that green gate?

"Good-bye," he said, "and please forget all the rot I talked about Jericho. It goes with the spade and bucket, and all the rest. You have been most awfully kind to me, all along. But the very kindest thing you can do now, is to forget all the impossible things I thought and said... Allow me.... I'll shut the door."

He put up his hand, to lift his cap; but he was bareheaded. He laughed again; turned, and passed out.

70

"Boy! Boy! Come back," said Christobel. But the door had closed on the first word.

She stood alone.

This time she did not wait. Where was the good of waiting?

She turned and walked slowly up the lawn, pausing to look at the flowers in the border. The yellow roses still looked golden. The jolly little "what-d'-you-call-'ems" lifted pale purple faces to the sky.

But the Boy was gone.

She reached her chair, where he had placed it, deep in the shade of the mulberry-tree. She felt tired; worn-out; old.

The Boy was gone.

She leaned back with closed eyes. She had hurt him so. She remembered all the glad, sweet confident things he had said each day. Now she had hurt him so.... What radiant faith, in love and in life, had been his. But she had spoiled that faith, and dimmed that brightness.

Suddenly she remembered his dead mother's prayer for him. "I have prayed for thee, that thy faith fail not." And under those words she had written "Christobel." Would he want to obliterate that name? No, she knew he would not. Nothing approaching a hard or a bitter thought could ever find a place in his heart. It would always be the golden heart of her little Boy Blue.

Tears forced their way beneath her closed lashes, and rolled slowly down her cheeks.

"Oh, Boy dear," she said aloud, "I love you so—I love you so!"

"I know you do, dear," he said. "It's almost unbelievable—yet I know you do."

She opened her eyes. The Boy had come back. She had not heard his light step, on the springy turf. He knelt in his favourite place, on the left of her chair, and bent over her. Once more his face was radiant. His faith had not failed.

She looked up into his shining eyes, and the joy in her own heart made her dizzy.

"Boy dear," she whispered, "not my lips, because—I am not altogether yours—I may have to—you know?—the Professor. But, oh Boy, I can't help it! I'm afraid I care terribly."

He was quite silent; yet it seemed to her that he had shouted. A burst of trumpet-triumph seemed to fill the air.

He bent lower. "Of course I wouldn't, Christobel," he said; "not before the seventh day. But there's a lot beside lips, and it's all so dear."

Then she felt the Boy's kisses on her hair, on her brow, on her eyes. "Dear eyes," he said, "shedding tears for my pain. Ah, dear eyes!" And he kissed them again.

She put up her hand, to push him gently away. He captured it, and held it to his lips.

"Stop, Boy dear," she said. "Be good now, and sit down."

He slipped to the grass at her feet, and rested his head against her knee.

She stroked his hair, with gentle, tender touch. Her Little Boy Blue

72

had come back to her. Oh, bliss unutterable! Why worry about the future?

"How silly we were, dear!" he said. "How silly to suppose we could part like that—you and I!" Then his sudden merry laugh rang out— oh, such music! such sweet music! "I say, Christobel," he said, "it is all very well now to say 'Stop, and be good.' But on the seventh day, when the walls fall down, and I march up into the citadel, I shall give you millions of kisses—or will it be billions?"

"Judging from my knowledge of you, Boy dear," she said, "I rather think it would be billions."

Later, as they stood once more by the postern gate, he turned, framed in the doorway, smiling a last gay good-bye.

It was their second parting that day, and how different from the first. There was to be a third, unlike either, before the day was over; but its approach was, as yet, unsuspected.

But as he stood in the doorway, full in a shaft of sunlight, the glad certainty in his eyes smote her with sudden apprehension.

"Oh, Boy dear," she said, "take care! You are building castles again. They will tumble about our ears. I haven't promised you anything, Little Boy Blue of mine; and I am afraid I shall have to marry the Professor."

"If you do, dear," he said, "I shall have to give him a new umbrella as a wedding present!" And the Boy went whistling down the lane.

But, out of sight of the postern gate and of the woman who, leaning against it, watched him to the turning, he dropped his bounding step and jaunty bearing. His face grew set and anxious; his walk, perplexed.

"Oh, God," said the Boy, as he walked, "don't let me lose her!"

A few minutes later, a telegram was put into his hand from the friend left on the coast, in charge of his newest aeroplane.

"Arrange Channel flight, if possible, day after to-morrow."

"Not I," said the Boy, crumpling the message into his pocket. "The day after to-morrow is the seventh day."

He was dining with friends, but an unaccountable restlessness seized him during the evening. He made his excuses, and returned to the Bull Hotel soon after nine o'clock. The hall-porter at once handed him a note, left by special messenger, ten minutes earlier. It was marked "urgent." The handwriting was Christobel's.

The Boy flung away his cigarette, tore the note open, and turned to a light. It was very short and clear.

"Boy dear,—I must see you at once. You will find me in the garden.

"Christobel."

When the Boy had turned the corner and disappeared, Miss Charteris passed through the little postern gate, and moved slowly up the lawn. Ah, how different to her sad return from that gate an hour before!

The William Allen Richardsons still opened their golden hearts to the sunset. The jolly little "what-d'-you-call-'ems" still lifted their purple faces to the sky. But instead of stabbing her with agony, they sang a fragrant psalm of love.

Ah, why was the Boy so dear? Why was the Boy so near? She had watched him go striding down the lane, yet he still walked beside

74

her; his gay young laugh of glad content was in her ears; his pure young kisses on her brow and eyes; his head against her knee.

Just as she reached the mulberry, Jenkins hastened from the house. The note he brought, in a familiar handwriting, thin and pointed, was marked "urgent" in one corner, and "immediate" in the other; but Miss Ann's notes usually were one or other. This happened to be both.

"You need not wait, Jenkins," she said.

She stood close to a spreading branch of the mulberry. Her tall head was up among the moving leaves. Whispering, they caressed her. Something withheld her from entering the soft shade, sacred to herself and the Boy. She stood, to read Ann Harvey's letter.

As she read, every vestige of colour left her face. Bending over the letter, she might have been a sorely troubled and perplexed replica of the noble Venus of Milo.

Folding the letter, she went slowly up the lawn, still wearing that white look of cold dismay. She spoke to Martha through the open window, keeping her face out of sight.

"Martha," she said, "I am obliged to go immediately to Miss Ann. If I am not back by eight o'clock, I shall be remaining with her for dinner." She passed on, and Martha turned to Jenkins.

By the way, Jenkins was having an unusually festive time. During the last twenty-four hours, Martha had been kinder to him than he had ever known her to be. He was now comfortably ensconced in the Windsor armchair in a corner of the kitchen, reading yesterday's daily paper, and enjoying his pipe. Never before had his pipe been allowed in the kitchen; but he had just been graciously told he might bring it in, if he wouldn't be "messy with the hashes"; Mrs. Jenkins volunteering the additional remarkable information, that it was "good for the beetles." Jenkins was doubtful as to whether this meant that his pipe gave pleasure to the beetles, or the reverse; but experience had taught him that a condition of peaceful uncertainty in his own mind was to be preferred to a torrent of vituperative explanation from Martha. He therefore also received in silence the apparently unnecessary injunction not to go "crawlin' about all over the floor"; it took "a figure to do that!"

Eight o'clock came, and Miss Charteris had not returned.

"Remaining with 'er for dinner," pronounced Martha, flinging open the oven, and wrathfully relegating to the larder the chicken she had been roasting with extreme care; "an' a precious poor dinner it'll be! Jenkins, you may 'ave this sparrow-grass. I 'aven't the 'eart. An' me 'oping she'd 'ave 'ad the sense to keep 'im to dinner; knowing as there was a chicking an' 'grass for two. Now what's took Miss Hann 'urgent and immediate,' I'd like to know!" continued Martha, deriving considerable comfort from banging the plates and tumblers on to the kitchen table, with just as much violence as was consistent with their personal safety, as she walked round it, laying the table for supper. "Ate a biscuit, I should think, an' flown to 'er cheat. I've no patience; no, that I 'aven't!" And Martha attacked the loaf, with fury.

At a quarter before nine, Miss Charteris returned. In a few moments the bell summoned Jenkins. The note he was to take was also marked "Immediate." He left it on the kitchen table, and, while he changed his coat, Martha fetched her glasses. Then she followed him to the pantry.

"'Ere, run man!" she said, "run! Never mind your muffler. Who wants a muffler in June? 'E's in it! It's something more than a biscuit. Drat that woman!"

A quarter of an hour later, a tall white figure moved noiselessly down the lawn, to the seats beneath the mulberry. The full moon was just rising above the high red wall, gliding up among the trees, huge and golden through their branches. Christobel Charteris waited in the garden for the Boy.

He came.

By then, the lawn was bathed in moonlight. She saw him, tall and slim, in the conventional black and white of a man's evening dress, pass silently through the postern gate. She noted that he did not bang it. He came up the lawn slowly—for him. He wore no hat, and every clear-cut feature of the clean-shaven young face showed up in the moonlight.

At the mulberry, he paused, uncertain; peering into the dark shadow.

"Christobel?" he said, softly.

"Boy dear; I am here. Come."

He came; feeling his way among the chairs, and moving aside a table, which stood between.

He found her, sitting where he had found her, on his return, three hours before. A single ray of moonlight pierced the thick foliage of the mulberry, and fell across her face. He marked its unusual pallor. He stood before her, put one hand on each arm of her chair, and bent over her.

"What is it?" he said, softly. "What is it, dear heart? It is so wonderful to be wanted, and sent for. But let me know quickly that you are not in any trouble."

She looked up at him dumbly, during five, ten, twenty seconds. Then she said: "Boy, I have something to tell you. Will you help me to tell it?"

"Of course I will," he said. "How can I help best?"

"I don't know," she answered. "Oh, I don't know!"

He considered a moment. Then he sat down on the grass at her feet, and leaned his head against her knees. She passed her fingers softly through his hair.

"What happened after I had gone?" asked the Boy.

"Jenkins brought me a note from Miss Harvey, asking me to come to her at once, to hear some very wonderful news, intimately affecting herself, and the Professor, and—and me. She wrote very ecstatically and excitedly, poor dear. She always does. Of course, I went."

"Well?" said the Boy, gently. The pause was so very long, that it seemed to require supplementing. He felt for the other hand, which had been holding the lace at her breast, and drew it to his lips. It was wet with tears.

The Boy started. He sat up; turned, resting his arm upon her lap, and tried to see her face.

"Go on, dear," he said. "Get it over."

"Boy," said Miss Charteris, "a rich old uncle of the Harveys has died, leaving the Professor a very considerable legacy, sufficient to make him quite independent of his fellowship, and of the production of the Encyclopedia."

"Well?"

"They are very happy about it, naturally. Poor Ann is happier than I have ever seen her. And the chief cause of their joy appears to be that now the Professor is, at last, in a position to marry."

"Well?"

"I have not seen him yet, but Miss Ann is full of it. She told me a good many very touching things. I had no idea it had meant so much—to him—all these years.—Boy dear?"

"Yes."

"I shall have to marry the Professor."

No answer.

"I don't know how to make you understand why I feel so bound to them. They were very old friends of my father and mother. They were so good to me through all the days of sorrow, when I was left alone. Miss Ann is a great invalid, and very dependent upon love and care, and upon not being thwarted in her little hopes and plans. She expects to come and live in—in her brother's home. She knows I should love to have her. And he has done so much for me, intellectually; so patiently kept my mind alive, when it was inclined to stagnate; and working, when it would have grown slack. He has given up hours of his valuable time to me, every week, for years."

No answer.

Suddenly the moonlight, through an opening in the mulberry
79

leaves, fell upon his upturned face. She saw the anguish in his eyes. She turned his head away, resting it against her knee, and clasped her hands upon it.

"Boy dear; it is terribly hard for us, I know. In a most extraordinary way—in a way I cannot understand—you have won my body. It yearns to be with you; it aches if you suffer; it lives in your gladness; it grows young in your youth. Nobody else has ever made me feel this; I do not suppose anybody else ever will. But—oh Boy—bodies are not everything. Bodies are the least of all. And I think—I think the Professor holds my mind. He won it long ago. I have grown much older since then, and very tired of waiting. But I can look back to the time when I used to think the greatest privilege in the world would be, to be the—to marry the Professor."

She paused, and waited.

"Bodies count," said the Boy, in a low voice. "You'll jolly well find, that bodies count."

It was such a relief to hear him speak at last.

"Oh, I know, Boy dear," she said. "But more between some, than others. The Professor and I are united, primarily, on the mental and spiritual plane. Being so sure of this, realizing the difference, makes it less hard, in a way, to—to give up my Little Boy Blue. Boy dear, you must help me; because I love you as I have never loved anybody else in this world before; as I know I never shall love again. But I am bound in honour not to disappoint the man who knows I have waited for him. Miss Ann admitted to me to-night that she has told him. She said, in the first moments of joy she had to tell him; he was so anxious; and so diffident. Boy dear, had it not been for that, I think I should have begged off. But—as he knows—

as they have trusted me—dear, we must say 'good-bye' to-night. He is going to write to me to-morrow, asking if he may come. I shall say: 'Yes.' ... Boy dear? Is it very hard? ... Oh, can't you see where duty comes in? There can be no true happiness if one has failed to be true to what one knows is just and right.... Can't you realize, Boy, that they have been everything to me for seven years? You have come in, for seven days."

"Time is nothing," said the Boy, suddenly. "You and I are one, Christobel; eternally, indissolubly one. You will find it out, when it is too late. Age is nothing! Time is nothing! Love is all!"

She hesitated. The Boy's theories were so vital, so vigorous, so assured. Was she making a mistake? There was no question as to the pain involved by her decision; but was that pain to result as she believed, in higher good to all; or was it to mean irreparable loss? The very knowledge that her body so yearned for him, led her to emphasize the fact that the Boy could not—oh surely could not—be a fit mate for her mind. Yet he was so confident, so sure of himself, in regard to her, on every point; so unhesitatingly certain that they were meant for each other.

And then she saw Ann Harvey, with clasped hands, saying: "Darling child, forgive me, but I had to tell Kenrick! He is so humble—he was so diffident, so doubtful of his own powers of attraction. I had to tell him that I knew you had been very fond of him for years. I did not say much, sweet child; but just enough to give dear Kenrick hope and confidence."

She could see Miss Ann's delicate wrinkled face; the tearful eyes; the lavender ribbons on her lace cap; the mysterious hair-brooch, fastening the old lace at her neck. The scene was photographed upon her memory; for, in that moment, Hope—the young Hope,

81

born of the youthful Boy and his desires—had died. Christobel Charteris had taken up the burden of life; a life apart from the seven days' romance, created by the amazing over-confidence of her Little Boy Blue.

The masterful man attracts; but, in the end, it is usually the diffident man who wins. The innate unselfishness of the noblest type of woman, causes her to yield more readily to the insistence of her pity than to the force of her desire. In these cases, marriage and martyrdom are really—though unconsciously—synonymous; and the same pure, holy courage which went smiling to the stake, goes smiling to the altar. Does a martyr's crown await it, in another world? Possibly. The only perplexing question, in these cases, being: What awaits the wrecked life of "the other man"?

Christobel Charteris had put her hand to the plough; she would not look back.

"Little Boy Blue," she said, "you must say 'good-bye' and go. I am going to marry the Professor quite soon, and I must not see you again. Say 'good-bye,' Boy dear."

Then the Boy's anguish broke through all bounds. He flung his arms around her, and hid his face in her lap. A sudden throb of speechless agony seemed to overwhelm them both, submerging all arguments, all casuistry, all obligations to others, in a molten ocean of love and pain.

Then she heard the Boy pray: "O God, give her to me! Give her to me! O God, give her to me!"

"Hush, Boy," she said; "oh, hush!"

He was silent at once.

Then bending, she gathered him to her, holding his face against her breast; sheltering him in the tenderness of her arms. He had never seemed so completely her own Little Boy Blue as in that moment, when she listened to his hopeless prayer: "O God, give her to me!" This was the Little Boy Blue who tried to carry cannon-balls; who faced the world, with sand upon his nose; cloudless faith in his bright eyes; indomitable courage in his heart. She forgot the man's estate to which he had attained; she forgot the man's request to which she had given a final denial. She held him as she had first longed to do, when his nurse, in unreasonable wrath, shook him on the sands; she rocked him gently to and fro, as his dead mother might have done, long years ago. "Oh, my Little Boy Blue, my Little Boy Blue!" she said.

Suddenly she felt the Boy's hot tears upon her neck.

Then, in undreamed of pain, her heart stood still. Then the full passion of her tenderness awoke, and found voice in an exceeding bitter cry.

"Oh, I cannot bear it! I cannot bear it! Boy dear, oh, Boy dear, you shall have all you wish—all—all! ... Do you hear, my Little Boy Blue? It shall all be for you, darling; all for you! Nobody else matters. You shall have all you want—all—all—all!"

Silence under the mulberry-tree; the silence of a great decision.

Then he drew himself gently but firmly from her arms.

He stood before her, tall, erect, unbending. The moonlight fell upon his face. It had lost its look of youth, taking on a new power. It was the face of a man; and of a man who, having come to a decision, intended, at all costs, to abide by it.

"No, Christobel," he said. "No, my Belovèd. I could not accept happiness—even such happiness—at so great a cost to you. There could be no bliss for you, no peace, no satisfaction, even in our great love, if you had gone against your supreme sense of duty; your own high conception of right and wrong. Also, Christobel, dearest—you must not give yourself in a rush of emotion. You must give yourself deliberately where your mind has chosen, and where your great soul is content. That being so, I must be off, Christobel; and don't you worry about me. You've been heavenly good to me, dear; and I've put you through so much. I will go up to town to-night. I shall not come back, unless you send for me. But when you want me and send—why, my Love, I will come from the other end of the world."

He stooped and took both her hands in his; lifted them reverently, tenderly, to his lips; held them there one moment, then laid them back upon her lap, and turned away.

She saw him walk down the moonlit lawn, tall and erect. She saw him pass through the gate, without looking back. She heard it close quietly—not with the old boyish bang—yet close irrevocably, decisively.

Then she shut her eyes, and began again to rock gently to and fro. Little Boy Blue was still in her arms; it comforted her to rock him there. But the man who had arisen and left her, when he might, taking advantage of her weakness, have won her against her own conscience and will; the man who, mastering his own agony, had thus been brave and strong for her—had carried her whole heart with him, when he went out through the postern gate.

In rising, he left the Boy in her arms. Through the long hard years

84

to come, she prayed she might keep him there—her own Little Boy Blue.

But he who went out alone, for her sake to face life without her, was the man she loved.

She knew it, at last.

"And the evening and the morning were the fifth day."

THE SIXTH DAY

MISS ANN HAS "MUCH TO SAY"

On the afternoon of the sixth day, at the hour which had hitherto been kept for the Boy, Christobel Charteris, in response to another urgent and immediate summons, went to take tea with Miss Ann.

It had been a long, dull, uneventful day, holding at first a certain amount of restless uncertainty as to whether the Boy was really gone; mingled with apprehensive anticipation of a call from the Professor.

But before noon a reply-paid telegram arrived from the Boy, sent off at Charing Cross.

"Good morning. All's well. Just off for Folkestone. Please tell me how you are."

To which, while Jenkins and the telegraph-boy waited, Miss Charteris replied:

"Quite well, thank you. Do be careful at Folkestone."

and afterwards thought of many other messages which she might have sent, holding more, and better expressed. But that precious moment in touch with the Boy passed so quickly; and it seemed so impossible to think of anything but commonplace words, while Jenkins stood at attention near the table; and the telegraph-boy kept ringing his bicycle-bell outside, as a reminder that he waited.

Yet her heart felt warmed and comforted by this momentary contact with the Boy. He still cared to know how she was. And it was so like him to put: "All's well." He wished her to know he had not gone down beneath his trouble. "Fanks, but I always does my own cawwying." Brave Little Boy Blue, of long ago!

The expectation of the Professor's note or call remained, keeping her anxious; until she heard from Ann Harvey, that her brother had been obliged to go to London on business, and would not return until the evening. "Come to tea with me, dear child," the note concluded; "we have much to say!"

It seemed to Christobel that there remained nothing which Miss Ann had not already said, in every possible form and way. Nevertheless, she put on her hat, and went. Miss Ann had succeeded in impressing all her friends with the conviction that her wishes must never be thwarted.

Miss Ann had named her villa "Shiloh," undoubtedly a suitable name, so far as she herself was concerned; her time being mostly spent upon a comfortable sofa in her tiny drawing-room; or reclining on a wicker lounge beneath the one tree in her small garden; or being carefully wheeled out in a bath-chair.

But nobody else found Miss Ann's villa in any sense a "resting-place." She had a way of keeping everybody about her—from jaded Emma to the most casual caller—on the move, while she herself presented a delicate picture of frail inactivity. Immediately upon their arrival, her friends found an appointed task awaiting them; but it was always something which Miss Ann would have given to somebody else to do, had they not chanced at that moment to appear; and they were usually left with the feeling that the particular somebody else—whose privilege they, in their well-meant zeal, had usurped—would have accomplished it better.

Directing them from the sofa, Miss Ann kept her entourage busy and perpetually on the move. Yet she never felt she was asking much of them; nor, however weary at the conclusion of the task, did they ever feel much had been accomplished, owing to the judicious use of the word "just."

"My dear," Miss Ann would say, "as you are here, will you just clean the canary?" Cleaning the canary meant a very thorough turning out of an intricate little brass cage; several journeys up and down stairs in quest of sand, seed, and brass polish, and an outdoor excursion to a neighbour's garden for groundsel. The canary's name was "Sweetie-weet," and, however much annoyed Miss Ann's friends might be feeling with the canary, they had to call him "Sweetie-weet" all the time they "cleaned him," lest his flutterings should upset Miss Ann. Now you cannot say "Sweetie-weet" in an angry voice. Try, and you will see. Consequently Miss Ann's friends had no vent for their feelings during the process of getting a rather large hand in and out of a very small brass door with a spring, which always snapped to, at the wrong moment, while the hand, which seemed to its possessor larger than it had ever seemed before, was crooked round in an impossible position in a strained attempt to fix Sweetie-weet's perches. If anything went wrong during the cleaning process, Miss Ann, from her vantage-ground on the sofa would sigh, and exclaim: "Poor patient little Sweetie-weet!" Miss Ann was in full possession of all her faculties. Her hearing was preternaturally sharp. It was no use saying "Fiend!" to Sweetie-weet, in an emphatic whisper. He fluttered the more.

When the task was completed, the cage had to be brought to Miss Ann's couch for inspection. She then usually discovered the perches to have been put back before they were perfectly dry. Now nothing—as surely you hardly ought to require to be told—was so

88

prejudicial to Sweetie-weet's delicate constitution as to have damp wood beneath his precious little feet. Consequently all the perches had just to be taken out again, dried before the kitchen fire, and put back once more. When this mandate went forth, the glee in the bright black eyes in Sweetie-weet's yellow head was unmistakable. He shared Miss Ann's mania for keeping people busy.

When, at last, the second installation of perches was over, and the cage was suspended from the brass chain in the sunny window, Sweetie-weet poured forth a shrill crescendo of ear-piercing sarcasm—"a little song of praise" Miss Ann called it—directed full at the hot and exhausted friend, who was applying a pocket-handkerchief to the wire scratches on the back of her hand, and trying to smile at Miss Ann's recital of all Emma would say, when she found that her special privilege and delight—the cleaning of Sweetie-weet—had been wrested from her by the over-zealous friend. As a matter of fact, jaded Emma's personal remarks about Sweetie-weet, during the perch-drying process in the kitchen, had been of a nature which would not bear repeating in Sweetie-weet's presence, and had provided the only amusement the friend had got out of the whole performance.

When Christobel Charteris arrived at Shiloh, she found Miss Ann on the green velvet sofa, looking very frail and ethereal; a Shetland shawl about her shoulders, fastened by the largest and most mysterious of her hair-brooches—a gold-mounted oval brooch, in which a weeping willow of fair hair drooped over a sarcophagus of dark hair; while a crescent moon of grey hair kept watch over both. This funereal collection of family hair always possessed a weird fascination for small children, brought by their parents to call upon Miss Ann. The most undemonstrative became affectionate, and hastened with ready docility to the sofa to kiss Miss Ann, in order to obtain a closer view, and to settle the much disputed point as to the significance of a small round object in the left-hand corner at the bottom. In fact, to the undisguised dismay of his mother, a sturdy youngster once emerged from Miss Ann's embrace, exclaiming eagerly to his little sister: "It's a furze-bush, not a hedgehog!" An unfortunate remark, which might have been taken by Miss Ann to refer to even more personal matters than a detail in her brooch.

Christobel herself was not altogether free from the spell of this hirsute cemetery; chiefly because she knew it was worn on days when deep emotion was to be felt and expressed. At sight of it, she was quite prepared for the tearful smile with which Miss Ann signed to her to close the door. Then extending her arms, "Sweet sister," she said, with emotion, "let me take you to my heart."

It was somewhat startling to Christobel to be apostrophized as "sister" by Miss Ann. The Boy had made her feel so young, and so completely his contemporary, that if Miss Ann had called her "daughter," or even "granddaughter," it would have seemed more appropriate. Also her magnificent proportions constituted a somewhat large order for Miss Ann's proposed embrace.

However, she knelt beside the sofa, and allowed herself to be taken to Miss Ann's heart in sections. Then, having found and restored Miss Ann's lace pocket-handkerchief, she seated herself in a low chair beside the couch, hoping for enlightenment upon the immediate prospects of her own future.

Miss Ann wept gently for a while. Christobel sat silent. Her recent experience of tears, wrung from such deep anguish of soul, made it less easy for her to feel sympathetic towards tears which flowed from no apparent cause, and fell delicately into perfumed lace. So she waited in silence, while Miss Ann wept.

The room was very still. The bang with which the Boy usually made his entry anywhere, would have been terrific in its joyful suddenness. At the mere thought of it, Christobel's heart stood still and listened. But this was a place into which the Boy would never make an entry, noisy or otherwise. Besides—the Boy was gone. Oh, silent, sober, sorry world! The Boy was gone.

Sweetie-weet put his head on one side, and chirped interrogatively. In his judgment, the silence had lasted sufficiently long.

Miss Ann dried her eyes, making an effort to control her emotion. Then she spoke, in a voice which still trembled.

"Dearest child," she said, "I want you just to cover this book for me. Emma has offered to do it, several times, but I said: 'No, Emma. We must keep it for Miss Christobel. I do not know what she would say to you, if you took to covering my books!' Emma is a good soul, and willing; but has not the mind and method required to cover a book properly. If you will just run up to my room, dear child, you will find a neat piece of whity-brown paper laid aside on purpose.... Hush, Sweetie-weet! Christobel knows you are pleased to see her.... It is either on the ottoman behind the screen, or in the top left-hand drawer of the mahogany chest, between the window and the fireplace. Ah, how much we have come through, during the last twenty-four hours! The scissors, dear Love, are hanging by black tape from a nail in the store-room. You require a large and common pair for cutting brown paper. How truly wonderful are the ways of Providence, dear Christobel! The paste is in the little cupboard under the stairs."

When Miss Charteris had finished covering the book, having bent upon it all the mind and method it required, she forestalled the setting of another task, by saying firmly: "I want an important talk

91

now, please. Ann, are you sure you told your brother that I had cared for him for years?"

"Darling, dear Kenrick was so diffident; so unable to realize his own powers of attraction; so— —"

"Do you think it was fair toward a woman, even if it were true, to tell a man who had never asked her love, that that love has long been his?"

"Sweet child, how crudely you put it! I merely hinted, whispered; gave the most delicate indications of what I knew to be your feeling. For you do love my brother; do you not, dear Christobel?"

"I think," said Miss Charteris, slowly, weighing each word; "I think I love the Professor as a woman loves a book."

There was a moment of tense silence in Miss Ann's drawing-room. Christobel Charteris looked straight before her, a stern light upon her face, as of one confronted on the path of duty by the clear shining of the mirror of self-revelation.

Into Miss Ann's pale blue eyes shot a gleam of nervous anxiety.

Sweetie-weet chirped, interrogatively.

Then Miss Ann, recovering, clasped her hands. "Ah, what a beautiful definition!" she said. "What could be more pure, more perfect?"

Miss Charteris knew a love of a very different kind, which was absolutely pure, and altogether perfect. But that was the love she had put from her.

"A woman could hardly marry a book," she said.

Miss Ann gave a little deprecatory shriek. "Darling child!" she cried. "No simile, however beautiful, should be pressed too far! Your exquisite description of your love for dear Kenrick merely assures us that your union with him will prove one of complete contentment to the mind. And the mind—that sensitive instrument, attuned to all the immensities of the intellectual spheres—the mind is what really matters."

"Bodies count," said Miss Charteris, with conviction; adding beneath her breath, the dawning of a smile in her sad eyes: "We shall jolly well find, bodies count."

Miss Ann's hearing, as we have already remarked, was preternaturally sharp. She started. "My dear Christobel, what an expression! And do you not think, that, under these circumstances, any mention of bodies savours of impropriety?"

Miss Charteris turned quickly. The colour flamed into her beautiful face. The glint of angry indignation flashed from her eyes. But the elderly figure on the couch looked so small and frail. To wound and crush it would be so easy; and so unworthy of her strength, and wider experience.

Suddenly she remembered a little blue back, round with grief and shame; a small sandy face, silent and unflinching; a brave little heart which kept its faith in God, and prayed on trustfully, while nurses misunderstood and bullied. Then Miss Charteris conquered her own wrath.

"Dear Ann," she said, gently, "do you really believe your brother would be much disappointed if—after all—when he asks me to marry him—which he has not done yet—I feel it better not to do so?"

93

"My darling child!" exclaimed Miss Ann, and her hair-brooch flew open, as if to accentuate her horror and amazement. "My darling child! Think how patiently he has waited! Remember the long years! Remember——"

"Yes, I know," said Miss Charteris. "You told me all that last night, didn't you? But it seems to me that, if a man can wait twelve years, he might as well wait twenty."

"So he would have!" cried Miss Ann. "Undoubtedly dear Kenrick would have waited twenty years, had it not been for this fortunate legacy, which places him in a position to marry at once. But why should you wish to keep him waiting any longer? Is not twelve years sufficiently long?"

Miss Charteris smiled. "Twelve days would be too long for some people," she said, gently. "I have no wish to keep him waiting. But you must remember, Ann, the Professor has, as yet, spoken no word of love to me."

"Dear child," said Miss Ann, eagerly; "he would have come to you to-day, but imperative legal business, connected with our uncle's will, took him to town. I know for certain that he intends writing to you this evening; and, if you then give him leave to do so, he will call upon you to-morrow. Oh, darling girl, you will not disappoint us? We have so trusted you; so believed in you! A less scrupulously honourable man than Kenrick, might have tried to bind you by a promise, before he was in a position to offer you immediate marriage. Think of all the hopes—the hopes and p-plans, which depend upon your faithfulness!" Miss Ann dissolved into tears— but not to a degree which should hinder her flow of eloquence. "Ah, sweetest child! You knelt beside this very sofa, five years ago, and you said: 'Ann, I think any woman might be proud to become the wife of the Professor!' Have you forgotten that you said that, kneeling beside this very sofa?"

"I have not forgotten," said Miss Charteris; "and I think so still."

"Then you will marry Kenrick?" said Miss Ann, through her tears.

Christobel Charteris rose. She stood, for a moment, tall and immovable, in the small, low room, crowded with knick-knacks— china, bric-à-brac, ferns in painted pots, embroidery, photograph frames—overseated with easy chairs, which, in their turn, were overfilled with a varied assortment of cushions. Miss Ann's drawing-room gave the effect of a rather prettily arranged bazaar. You mentally pictured yourself walking round, admiring everything, but seeing nothing you liked quite well enough to wish to buy it, and take it home.

Christobel Charteris, tall and stately, in her simple white gown, looked so utterly apart from the trumpery elegance of these surroundings. As the Boy had said, the mellow beauty of his ancestral homes would indeed be a fit setting for her stately grace. But she had sent away the Boy, with his beautiful castles in the air, and places in the shires. The atmosphere and surroundings of Shiloh were those to which she must be willing to bend her fastidious taste. Miss Ann would expect to make her home with the Professor.

"Then you will marry Kenrick?" whispered Miss Ann, through her lace pocket-handkerchief.

Christobel bent over her, tenderly; fastening the clasp of the mysterious hair-brooch.

"Dear Ann," she said. "It will not be leap year again, until 1912.

And, meanwhile, the Professor has not proposed marriage to me."

Miss Ann instantly brightened. Laughing gaily, she wiped away a few remaining tears.

"Ah, naughty!" she said. "Naughty, to make me tell! But as you will ask—he is going to write to-night. But you must never let him know I told you! And now I want you just to find the Spectator—it is laid over that exquisitely embroidered blotter on the writing-table in the window, sent me last Christmas by that kind creature, Lady Goldsmith; so thoughtful, tasteful, and quite touching; Emma, careful soul, spread it over the blotter, while darling Sweetie-weetie took his bath. Dear pet, it is a sight to see him splash and splutter. Lady Goldsmith thinks so much of dear Kenrick. The first time she saw him, she was immensely struck by his extraordinarily clever appearance. He sat exactly opposite her at a Guildhall banquet; and she told me afterwards that the mere sight of him was sufficient to take away all inclination for food; excepting for that intellectual nourishment which he is so well able to supply. I thought that was rather well expressed, and, coming from a florid woman, such as Lady Goldsmith, was quite a tribute to my brother. You would call Lady Goldsmith 'florid,' would you not, dear Christobel? ... Oh, you do not know her by sight? I am surprised. As the wife of the Professor, you will soon know all these distinguished people by sight. Yes, she is undoubtedly florid; and inclined to be what my dear father used to call 'a woman of a stout habit.' This being the case, it was certainly a tribute—a tribute of which you and I, dearest child, have a right to feel justly proud.... Oh, is it still damp? Naughty Sweetie-weet! Don't you think it might be wise, just to take it to the kitchen. Emma, good soul, will let you dry it before the fire. I have heard of fatalities caused by damp newspapers. Precious child, we can have you run no risks! What would Kenrick say? But

96

when it is absolutely dry, I want you just to explain to me the gist of that article on the effect of oriental literature on modern thought. Kenrick tells me you have read it. He wishes to discuss it with me. I really cannot undertake to read it through. I have not the time required. Yet I must be prepared to talk it over intelligently with my brother, when next he pays me a visit. He may look in this evening, weary with his day in town, and requiring the relaxation of a little intellectual conversation. I must be ready."

An hour later, somewhat tired in body, and completely exhausted in mind, Miss Charteris walked home. She made a detour, in order to pass along the lane, and enter through the postern gate at the bottom of the garden.

She opened it, and passed in.

A shaft of sunlight lay along the lawn. The jolly little "what d'-you-call-'ems" lifted gay purple faces to the sky.

She paused in the doorway, trying to realize how this quiet green seclusion, the old-fashioned flower-borders, the spreading mulberry-tree, the quaint white house, in the distance, with its green shutters, must have looked to the Boy each day, as he came in. She knew he had more eye for colour, and more knowledge of artistic effect, than his casual acquaintances might suppose. It would not surprise her some day to find, as one of the gems of the New Gallery, a reproduction of her own garden, with a halo of jolly little "what-d'-you-call-'ems" in the borders, and an indication of seats, deep in the shadow of the mulberry-tree. She would not need to refer to the catalogue for the artist's name. The Boy had had a painting in the Academy the year before. She had chanced to see it. Noticing the name of her Little Boy Blue of the Dovercourt sands in the catalogue, she had made her way through the crowded rooms, and found his picture. It hung on the line. She had been struck by its thoughtful beauty, and wealth of imaginative skill. She had not forgotten that picture; and during all these days she had been quietly waiting to hear the Boy say he had had a painting in the Academy. Then she was going to tell him she had seen it, had greatly admired it, and had noted with pleasure all the kind things critics had said of it.

But, the subject of pictures not having come up, it had not occurred to the Boy to mention it. The Boy never talked of what he had done, because he had done it. But were a subject mentioned upon which he was keen, he would bound up, with shining eyes, and tell you all he knew about it; all he had seen, heard, and done; all he was doing, and all he hoped to do in the future, in connexion with that particular thing. He would never have thought of informing you that he owned three aeroplanes. But if the subject of aviation came up, and you said to the Boy: "Do you know anything about it?" he would lean forward, beaming at you, and say: "I should jolly well think I do!" and talk aeroplanes to you for as long as you were willing to listen. This trait of the Boy's, caused shallow-minded people to consider him conceited. But the woman he loved knew how to distinguish between keenness and conceit; between exuberant enthusiasm and egotistical self-assertion; and the woman who loved him, smiled tenderly as she remembered that even on the day when she scolded him, and he had to admit his "barely respectable B.A.," he had not told her of the painting hung on the line and mentioned in the Times. Yet if the question of art had come up, the Boy would very probably have sat forward in his chair, and talked about his painting, straight on end, for half an hour.

She still stood beneath the archway, in the red-brick wall, as these thoughts chased quickly through her mind. She would have made a fair picture for any one who had chanced to be waiting beneath the mulberry-tree, with eyes upon the gate.

"Straight on end for half an hour, he would have talked about his picture; and how bright his eyes would have been. And then I should have said: 'I saw it, Boy dear; and it was quite as beautiful as you say.' And he would have answered: 'It jolly well gave you the feeling of the scene, didn't it, Christobel?' And I should have known that his delight in it, as an artistic success, had nothing to do with the fact that it was painted by himself. Just because egotism is impossible to him, he is free to be so full of vivid enthusiasm."

She smiled again. A warm glow seemed to enfold her. "How well I know my Boy!" she said aloud; then remembered with a sudden pang that she must not call him her Boy. She had let him go. She was—very probably—going to marry the Professor. She had not—with the whole of her being—wanted him to stay, until he had had the manliness to rise up and go. Then—it had been too late. Ah, was it too late? If the Boy came back to plead once more? If once again she could hear him say: "Age is nothing! Time is nothing! Love is all!" would she not answer: "Yes, Guy. Love is all"?

The blood rushed into her sweet proud face. The name of the man she loved had come into her mind unconsciously. It had never yet—as a name for him—passed her lips. That she should unconsciously call him so in her heart, gave her another swift moment of self-revelation.

She closed the gate gently, careful not to let it bang. As she passed up the lawn, her heart stood still. It seemed to her that he must be waiting, in the shade of the mulberry-tree.

She hardly dared to look. She felt so sure he was there.... Yes, she knew he was there.... She felt certain the Boy had come back. He could not stay away from her on his sixth day. Had he not said he would "march round" every day? Ah, dear waiting army of Israel! Here was Jericho hastening to meet it. Why had she allowed Ann Harvey to keep her so late? Why had she gone at all, during the Boy's own time? She might have known he would come.... Should she walk past the mulberry, as if making for the house, just for the joy of hearing him call "Christobel"? No, that would not be quite honest, knowing he was there; and they were always absolutely honest with one another.

She passed, breathlessly, under the drooping branches. Her cheeks glowed; her lips were parted. Her eyes shone with love and expectation.

She lifted a hanging bough, and passed beneath.

His chair was there, and hers; but they were empty. The Boy — being the Boy — had not come back.

Presently she went slowly up to the house.

A telegram lay on the hall table. She knew at once from whom it came. There was but one person who carried on a correspondence by telegraph. Reply paid was written on the envelope.

She stood quite still for a moment. Then she opened it slowly. Telegrams from the Boy gave her a delicious memory of the way he used to jump about. He would be out of his chair, and sitting at her feet, before she knew he was going to move.

She opened it slowly, turned to a window, and read it.

"How are you, dear? Please tell me. I am going to do my big fly to-morrow. I jolly well mean to break the record. Wish me luck."

She took up the reply-paid form and wrote:

"Quite well. Good luck; but please be careful, Little Boy Blue."

She hesitated a moment, before writing the playful name by which she so often called him. But his telegram was so absolutely the Boy, all over. It was best he should know nothing of "the man she loved," who had gone out at the gate. It was best he should not know what she would have called him, had he been under the mulberry just now. She was—undoubtedly—going to marry the Professor. In which case she would never call the Boy anything but "Little Boy Blue." So she put it into her telegram, as a repartee to his audacious "dear." Then she went out, and sent it off herself. It was comforting to have something, however small, to do for him.

She came in again; dressed for the evening, and dined. She was thoroughly tired; and one sentence beat itself incessantly against the mirror of her reflection, like a frightened bird with a broken wing: "He is going to do a big fly to-morrow.... He is going to do a big fly to-morrow! Little Boy Blue is going to fly and break the record."

She sat in the stillness of her drawing-room, and tried to read. But between her eyes and the printed page, burned in letters of fire: "He is going to fly to-morrow."

She went down the garden to the chairs beneath the mulberry-tree. It was cooler there; but the loneliness was too fierce an agony.

She walked up and down the lawn, now bathed in silvery moonlight. "He is going to do a big fly to-morrow. He jolly well means to break the record."

She passed in, and went to her bedroom. She lay in the darkness
101

and tried to sleep. She tried in vain. What if he got into cross-currents? What if the propeller broke? What if the steering-gear twisted? She began remembering every detail he had told herself and Mollie; when she sat listening, thinking of him as Mollie's lover, though all the while he had been her — Little Boy Blue.... "Oh of course then it is all U P. — But there must be pioneers!"

At last she could bear it no longer. She lighted her candle, and rose. She went to her medicine cupboard, and did a thing she had never done before, in the whole of her healthy life. She took a sleeping draught. The draught was one of Miss Ann's; left behind at the close of a recent visit. She knew it contained chiefly bromide; harmless but effective.

She put out the light, and lay once more in darkness.

The bromide began to act.

The bird with the broken wing became less insistent.

The absent Boy drew near, and bent over, kneeling beside her.

She talked to him softly. Her voice sounded far away, and unlike her own. "Be careful, Little Boy Blue," she said. "You may jolly well — what an expression! — break the record if you like; but don't break yourself; because, if you do, you will break my heart."

The bromide was acting strongly now. The bird with the broken wing had gone. There was a strange rhythmical throbbing in her ears. It was the Boy's aeroplane; but it had started without him. She knew sleep was coming; merciful oblivion. Yet now she was too happy to wish to sleep.

The Boy drew nearer.

"Oh, Boy dear, I love you so," she whispered into the throbbing darkness; "I love you so."

"I know you do, dear," said the Boy. "It is almost unbelievable, Christobel; but I know you do."

Then she put up her arms, and drew him to her breast.

Thus the Boy—though far away—marched round.

"And the evening and the morning were the sixth day."

AN INTERLUDE

"AS A DREAM, WHEN ONE AWAKETH"

When Miss Charteris opened her eyes, the sun was streaming into her room. The sense of having slept heavily and unnaturally lay upon her. She had not heard Martha's entry; but her blinds were up, and the tea on the tray beside her bed was still fresh and hot.

She took a cup, and the after-effects of the bromide seemed to leave her.

She dressed, and went downstairs.

On the breakfast-table, beside her plate, lay the Professor's letter. When she had poured out her coffee and buttered her toast, she opened and read it.

The letter was exactly such as she had always dreamed the Professor would write, if he ever came to the point of making her a proposal. He touched on their long friendship; on how much it had meant to them both. He said he had often hoped for the possibility of a closer tie, but had not felt justified in suggesting it, until he was in a position to offer her a suitable home and income. This was now fortunately the case; therefore he hastened to write and plead his cause, though keenly conscious of how little there was in himself calculated to call forth in a woman the affection which it was his earnest hope and desire to win. She had trusted him as a friend, an intellectual guide and comrade, during many years. If she could now bring herself to trust him in a yet more intimate relation, he would endeavour never to disappoint or fail her.

104

The letter was signed:

"Yours in sincere devotion, "   KENRICK HARVEY."

A postscript requested to be allowed to call, at the usual hour, that afternoon, for a reply.

Miss Charteris wrote a brief note of thanks and appreciation, and gave the Professor leave to call at three.

The Professor called at three.

He knocked and rang, and fumbled long over the umbrella-stand in the hall. He seemed to be taking all the umbrellas out, and putting them back again.

At last he appeared at the door of the drawing-room, where Miss Charteris awaited him. He was very nervous. He repeated the substance of his letter, only rather less well expressed. He alluded to Miss Ann, and to the extreme happiness and pleasure to her of having Christobel as a sister. But he completely ignored, both in the letter and in conversation, Miss Ann's betrayal of Christobel's confidence. For this she was grateful to him.

As soon as the Professor, having floundered through the unusual waters of expressed sentiment, stepped out on to the high and dry path of an actual question, Miss Charteris answered that question in the affirmative, and accepted the Professor's offer.

He rose, and held her hand for a few moments, looking at her with great affection through his glasses, which did not at all impede the warmth of his regard; in fact, being powerful convex lenses, they magnified it. Then he kissed her rather awkwardly on the brow, and hurried back to his seat.

A somewhat strained silence would have followed, had not the Professor had an inspiration.

Drawing a book from his pocket, he looked at her as you look at a child for whom you have a delightful surprise in store.

"That—er—matter being satisfactorily settled, my dear Christobel," he said, "should we not find it decidedly—er—refreshing to spend an hour over our Persian translation?"

Miss Charteris agreed at once; but while the Professor read, translated, and expounded, expatiating on the interest and beauty of various passages, her mind wandered.

She found herself picturing the Boy under similar circumstances; how the Boy would have behaved during the first hour of engagement; what the Boy would have said; what the Boy would have done. She was not quite sure what the Boy would have done; she had never experienced the Boy with the curb completely off. But she suddenly remembered: "Millions, or would it be billions?" and the recollection gave her a shock of such vivid reaction, that she laughed aloud.

The Professor paused, and looked up in surprise. Then he smiled, indulgently.

"My dear—er—Christobel, this passage is not intended to be humorous," he said.

"I know it is not," replied Miss Charteris. "I beg your pardon. I laughed involuntarily."

The Professor resumed his reading.

No; she was not quite sure as to all the Boy would have done; but she knew quite well what he would have said.

And here the Boy, quite unexpectedly, took a First in classics; for what the Boy would have said would certainly have been Greek to the Professor.

After this, events followed one another so rapidly that the whole thing became dream-like to Miss Charteris. She found herself helpless in the grip of Miss Ann's iron will—up to now, carefully shrouded in Shetland and lace. At last she understood why Emma's old mother had had to die alone in a little cottage away in Northumberland; Emma, good soul, being too devoted to her mistress to ask for the necessary week, in order to go home and nurse her mother. Emma had seemed a broken woman, ever since; and Christobel understood now the impossibility of any one ever asking Miss Ann for a thing which Miss Ann had made up her mind not to grant.

She and the Professor now became puppets in Miss Ann's delicate hands. Miss Ann lay upon her couch, and pulled the wires. The Professor danced, because he had not the discernment to know he was dancing; Miss Charteris, because she had not the heart to resist. The Boy having gone out of her life, nothing seemed to matter. It was her duty to marry the Professor, and there is nothing to be gained by the postponement of duty.

But it was Miss Ann who insisted on the wedding taking place within a week. It was Miss Ann who reminded them that, the Long Vacation having just commenced, the Professor could easily be away, and there were researches connected with his Encyclopedia which it was of the utmost importance he should immediately make in the museums and libraries of Brussels. It was Miss Ann who insisted upon a special licence being obtained, and who overruled Christobel's desire to be married by her brother, the bishop. Miss Ann had become quite hysterical at the idea of the bishop being brought back from a tour he was making in Ireland, and Christobel yielded the more readily, because her brother's arrival would undoubtedly have meant Mollie's; and Mollie's presence, even if she refrained from protest and expostulation, would have brought such poignant memories of the Boy.

So it came to pass, with a queer sense of the whole thing being dream-like and unreal, that Miss Charteris—who should have had the most crowded and most popular wedding in Cambridge—found herself standing, as a bride, beside the Professor, in an ill-ventilated church, at ten o'clock in the morning, being married by an old clergyman she had never seen before, who seemed partially deaf, and partially blind, and wholly inadequate to the solemn occasion; with Miss Ann and her faithful Emma, sniffing in a pew on one side; while Jenkins breathed rather heavily in a pew, on the other. Martha had flatly refused to attend; and when Miss Charteris sent for her to bid her good-bye, Martha had appeared, apparently in her worst and most morose temper; then had suddenly broken down, and, exclaiming wildly: "'Ow about 'im?" had thrown her apron over her head, and left the room, sobbing.

"How about him? How about him?"

Each turn of the wheels reiterated the question as she drove to Shiloh to pick up Miss Ann; then on to the church where the Professor waited.

How about him? But he had left her to do that which she felt to be right, and she was doing it.

Nevertheless, Martha's wild outburst had brought the Boy very near; and he seemed with her as she walked up the church.

Her mind wandered during the reading of the exhortation. In this

108

nightmare of a wedding she seemed to have no really important part to play. The Boy would burst in, in a minute; and a shaft of light would come with him. He would walk straight up the church to her, saying: "We have jolly well had enough of this, Christobel!" Then they would all wake up, and he would whirl her away in a motor and she would say: "Boy dear; don't exceed the speed-limit."

But the Boy did not burst in; and the Professor's hands, looking unusually large in a pair of white kid gloves, were twitching nervously, for an emphatic question was being put to him by the old clergyman, who had emerged from his hiding-place behind the Prayer-book, as soon as the exhortation was over.

The Professor said: "I will," with considerable emotion; while Miss Ann sobbed audibly into her lace pocket-handkerchief.

Christobel looked at the Professor. His outward appearance seemed greatly improved. His beard had been trimmed; his hair—what there was of it—cut. He had not once looked at her since she entered the church and took her place at his side; but she knew, if he did look, his eyes would be kind—kind, with a magnified kindness, behind the convex lenses. The Boy had asked whether she loved the Professor's mouth, eyes, and hair. What questions the amazing Boy used to ask! And she had answered— —

But here a silence in the church recalled her wandering thoughts. The all-important question had been put to her. She had not heard one word of it; yet the church awaited her "I will."

The silence became alarming. This was the exact psychological moment in which the Boy should have dashed in to the rescue. But the Boy did not dash in.

Then Christobel Charteris did a thing perhaps unique in the annals of brides, but essentially characteristic of her extreme honesty.

109

"I am sorry," she said, in a low voice; "I did not hear the question. Will you be good enough to repeat it?"

Miss Ann, in the pew behind, gasped audibly. The old clergyman peered at her, in astonishment, over his glasses. His eyes were red-rimmed and bloodshot.

Then he repeated the question slowly and deliberately, introducing a tone of reproof, which made of it a menace. Miss Charteris listened carefully to each clause and at the end she said: "I will."

Whereupon, with much fumbling, the Professor and the old clergyman between them, succeeded in finding a ring, and in placing it upon the third finger of her left hand. As they did so, her thoughts wandered again. She was back in the garden with the Boy. He had caught her left hand in both his, and kissed it; then, dividing the third finger from the others, and holding it apart with his strong brown ones, he had laid his lips upon it, with a touch of unspeakable reverence and tenderness. She understood now, why the Boy had kissed that finger separately. She looked down at it. The Professor's ring encircled it.

Then the old clergyman said: "Let us pray"; and, kneeling meekly upon her knees, Christobel Charteris prayed, with all her heart, that she might be a good wife to her old friend, the Professor.

From the church, they drove straight to the station, Miss Ann's plan for them being, that they should lunch in London, reach Folkestone in time for tea, and spend a day or two there, at a boarding-house kept by an old cronie of Miss Ann's, before crossing to Boulogne, en route for Brussels.

Christobel disliked the idea of the boarding-house, extremely. She had never, in her life, stayed at a boarding-house; moreover it

110

seemed to her that a wedding journey called imperatively for hotels—and the best of hotels. But Miss Ann had dismissed the question with an authoritative wave of the hand, and a veiled insinuation that hotels—particularly Metropole hotels—were scarcely proper places. Dear Miss Slinker's boarding-house would be so safe and nice, and the company so congenial. But here the Professor had interposed, laying his hand gently on Christobel's: "My dear Ann, we take our congenial company with us."

This was the farthest excursion into the realm of sentiment, upon which the Professor had as yet ventured. The sober, middle-aged side of Miss Charteris had appreciated it, with a certain amount of grateful emotion. But the youthful soul of Christobel had suddenly realized how the Boy would slap his leg, and rock, over the recital of such a sentence; and, between the two, she had been reduced to a condition bordering on hysterics.

They travelled from Cambridge in a first-class compartment, had it to themselves, and fell quite naturally into the style of conversation which had always characterized their friendship; meeting each other's minds, not over the happenings of a living present, but in a mutual appreciation of the great intellects of a dead and gone past. Before long, the Professor had whisked his favourite Persian poet from the tail-pocket of his coat, Christobel had provided paper and pencil, and they were deep in translation.

Arrived at Liverpool Street station, they entered a four-wheeler, and trundled slowly off to Cannon Street. Christobel had imagined four-wheelers to be obsolete; but the Professor dismissed her suggestion of a taxi, as being "a needlessly rapid mode of progression, indubitably fraught with perpetual danger," and proceeded to hail the sleepy and astonished driver of a four-wheeled cab.

(Oh, Boy dear, what would you have said to that four-wheeler—you dear record-breaking, speed-limit-exceeding, astonishingly rapid Boy? That ancient four-wheeler, trundling past the Bank of England, the Royal Exchange, the Mansion House, up King William Street, and round into Cannon Street, endlessly blocked, continually pulling up; then starting on, only to be stopped again; and your Belovèd inside it, Boy dear, looking out of the ramshackle old window, in a vain endeavour to see something of the London you had planned to show her in your own delightful extravagant way. Oh, Boy dear, keep out of this! It is not your show. This four-wheeler has been hailed and engaged by the Professor. The lady within is the bride of the Professor. Hands off, Boy!)

They drew up, for a few minutes, outside a bookseller's in New Broad Street, on the left-hand side, just after they had trundled into it—a delightful little place, crammed, lined, almost carpeted, with books. The Professor plunged in, upsetting a pile of magazines in his hasty entrance through the narrow doorway. Here he always found precisely the book he happened to be requiring for his latest research. With an incoherent remark to the proprietor, who advanced to meet him, the Professor became immediately absorbed, in a far corner of the shop, oblivious of his cab, his bride, and his train. Christobel had followed him, and stood, a dignified, but somewhat lonely figure, just within the doorway. She had been to this shop with her father, during his lifetime, on several occasions, and had since often written for books. The bookseller came forward. He was a man possessed of the useful faculty of remembering faces and the names appertaining to them. Also he had cultivated the habit of taking an intelligent interest in his customers. But he did not connect this beautiful waiting figure, with the absorbed back of the Professor.

"What can I do for you to-day, Miss Charteris?" he inquired, with ready courtesy.

Christobel started. "Nothing to-day, thank you, Mr. Taylor. But I am much obliged to you for so often supplying my requirements by return of post. And, by the way, you have an excellent memory. It is many years since I came here last, with my father."

"Professor Charteris was one of my best customers," said the bookseller, in an undertone of deferential sympathy. "I never knew a finer judge of a book than he. If I may be allowed to say so, I deeply deplored his loss, Miss Charteris."

Christobel smiled, and gently unbent, allowing the kindly expression of appreciation and regret to reach her with comfort in these moments of dream-like isolation. A friendly hand seemed to have been outstretched across the chasm which divides the passionately regretted past, from the scarcely appreciated present. She could see her father's tall scholarly figure, as he stood lovingly fingering a book, engaged in earnest conversation with Mr. Taylor, regardless of the passing of time; until she was obliged to lay her hand on his arm, and hurry him through the crowded streets, down the steep incline, to the platform from which the Cambridge express was on the point of starting. And when safely seated, with barely a minute to spare, he would turn to her, with a smile of gentle reproof, saying: "But, my dear child, we had not concluded our conversation." And she would laugh and say: "But we had to get home to-night, Papa." Whereupon he would lean back, contentedly, replying: "Quite right, my dear. So we had."

Ah, happy those whose fathers and mothers still walk the earth beside them. Youth remains, notwithstanding the passing of years, while there is still a voice to say, in reproof or approbation: "My child."

But the bookseller, not yet connecting her with the Professor, still waited her pleasure; and suddenly a thought struck Christobel. An eager wish awoke within her.

"Mr. Taylor," she said, hurriedly; "can you supply me with the very newest thing on the subject of aviation? I want to learn all there is to know about propellers, steering-gear, cross-currents, and how to avoid the dangers— —"

She stopped short. The Professor had found what he wanted, and was fumbling for his purse.

The bookseller turned quickly to a pile at his elbow, took up a paper-covered book, and placed it in her hands. "The very latest," he said. "Published yesterday. You will find in it all you want to know." Then, as he handed the Professor his change, "Allow me to place it to your account, Miss Charteris," he said.

Experiencing a quite unaccountable sense of elation and fresh interest in life, Christobel, armed with her book on aviation, re-entered the four-wheeler. The Professor, absorbed in his own purchase, had not noticed her private transaction. He followed her into the cab, and made three ineffectual attempts to close the door. Just as the driver was slowly beginning to prepare to climb down, Mr. Taylor came across the crowded pavement, to their rescue; released the Professor's coat-tail, shut them in, and signed to the cabman to drive on. With a good deal of "gee-up" and whip-flourishing, they re-commenced to trundle. Mr. Taylor was not merely a provider of literature; he was also a keen observer of life, and of human nature. As Christobel leaned forward to acknowledge his help, and to smile her farewell, his expression seemed to say: "A four-wheeler, Professor Harvey, and the latest work on aviation! An unusual combination." "Very unusual," she said to herself, and smiled again. Then it seemed to her that her friend of the bookshop had said: "You will find what you want, on page 274." She knew he had not, as a matter of fact, mentioned any page; but the figures came into her mind. She opened the book, and glanced at page 274. It was headed: "Fine performances by Mr. Guy Chelsea." She shut it quickly. There was no room for the actual presence of the Boy in the Professor's four-wheeler.

They lunched at a depôt of the Aerated Bread Company, close to Cannon Street station. While Christobel was struggling with a very large plateful of cold tongue, she suddenly remembered that one of the Boy's many plans had been to take her to lunch at his favourite restaurant in Piccadilly; where she would be able to order any dish she fancied, and find it better served than she had ever known it before; or to dine at the Hotel Metropole, where Monsieur Delma's perfect orchestra would play for her any mortal thing for which she chose to ask, and play it better than she had ever heard it played.

These memories, and a really excellent cup of coffee, helped Christobel in her struggles with the round of cold tongue; and she looked across the little marble-topped table brightly at the Professor, and spoke with a cheerful hopefulness which surprised herself.

But something, other than his own plate of cold tongue, seemed weighing on the Professor. He had become preoccupied and distrait.

When they reached the Folkestone train, Christobel found out the cause of his preoccupation.

"My dear Ann—I should say Christobel," remarked the Professor, hurriedly, as he put her into an empty compartment, and hesitated in the doorway. "I am always accustomed at this hour to have my pipe and a nap. Should you object, my dear Ann—er—that is, Christobel, if I sought a smoking compartment?"

"Oh, please do!" she exclaimed, eagerly. The idea of two hours of freedom and solitude suddenly seemed an undreamed of joy. "Don't think of me. I am quite happy here."

"I will provide you with a paper," said the Professor, and hailed a passing boy. He laid the paper on her lap, and disappeared.

The train started.

Christobel looked out of the window as they slowly steamed across the bridge over the Thames. She loved the flow of the river, with its constant procession of barges, dredges, boats, and steamers; a silent, moving highway, right through the heart of the noisy whirl of London street-traffic. They ran past old St. Saviour's Church, now promoted to be Southwark Cathedral; out through the suburbs, until streets became villas, woods and meadows appeared, and the train ran through Chislehurst—peaceful English resting-place where lie entombed the bright Imperial hopes of France—then on through Sevenoaks, into the bowery green of the Kentish hop-gardens.

After passing Sevenoaks, she took up the Professor's paper and glanced at it. Somehow she had felt sure it would be the Daily Graphic. It was the Daily Mirror! She had never held a halfpenny illustrated paper in her hands before. No doubt it was an excellent paper, and met the need of an immense number of people, to whom an additional halfpenny a day would be a consideration. But, that the Professor, when providing her with one paper, should have chosen a halfpenny instead of a penny paper, seemed to hold a

116

curious significance, and called up sudden swift memories of the Boy. He would have bought Punch, the Graphic, the Illustrated, the Spectator, and a Morning Post, plumped them all down on the seat in front of her; then sat beside her, and talked, the whole journey through, so that she would not have had a moment in which to open one of them.

(Oh, Boy dear! Don't look at this Daily Mirror. You might misjudge the good Professor. With your fifty thousand a year, how can you be expected to understand a mind which must consider ha'pence, even when brides and wedding journeys are concerned. Do keep away, Boy dear. This is not your wedding journey.)

Then she opened the Daily Mirror, and there looked out at her, from its central page, the merry, handsome, daring face of her own Little Boy Blue!

He was seated in his flying machine, steering-wheel in hand, looking out from among many wires. His cap was on the back of his head; his bright eyes looked straight into hers; his firm lips, parted in a smile, seemed to be saying: "I jolly well mean to do it." Beneath was an account of him, and a description of the flight he was to attempt on that day, across the Channel, circling round Boulogne Cathedral, and back. He was to start at two o'clock. At that very moment he must be in mid-air.

Oh, Little Boy Blue! Little Boy Blue! You have a way of making hearts stand still.

The boarding-house proved to be a place decidedly conducive to the taking of a fresh-air cure; because nobody remained within its four walls, if the weather could possibly admit of their going out.

117

As soon as Christobel and the Professor had taken tea, and replied to Miss Slinker's many questions, they went out to walk on the Leas until sunset. It was a radiant afternoon, and the strong wind which had suddenly arisen, blowing, in unexpected gusts, from the sea, acted as a tonic to weary heart and brain. Christobel, holding on her hat as she walked, battled her way beside the Professor, up a cross street, into the Sandgate Road.

There they went to the telegraph office, and sent Miss Ann news of their safe arrival, and of the extreme comfort they felt sure of experiencing at Miss Slinker's delightful abode. (This was the Professor's wording.)

They looked in at Parson's Library just to order a book Miss Ann wanted; and, on a little farther, just to match some crewel silks for a tea-cosy Miss Ann was making.

These commissions duly executed, they were free to make their way to the Leas parade, whence they would look down upon the beach, and enjoy a distance view across the Channel. They took the side street which brought them out upon the esplanade, close to the lift by which people continuously mounted or descended the steep face of the cliff.

A considerable crowd lined the esplanade railing, looking over eagerly. Apparently there was some object of particular interest to be seen below.

Christobel and the Professor advanced to the railing, and also looked over.

She saw a strange thing floating in the sea, between the promenade pier and the harbour. It seemed a huge insect, with broken wings. Its body was a mass of twisted wires. Around this, a little fleet of rowing-boats had gathered. They looked black, on the blue wind-swept waters, like water-boatmen on a village pond. They darted in and out and round about the wreckage of the huge wings and twisted wire, and seemed waiting for a chance to help.

A man stood next to Christobel and the Professor; a man who talked to himself.

"Ah, poor chap," he said; "poor chap! So nearly back! So nearly broke the record! Such a sport!"

"What is that thing in the water?" inquired the Professor.

The man turned and looked at him.

"An aeroplane," he said, slowly, speaking with a sort of stolid deliberation. "A wrecked aeroplane. Caught in a cross-current, worse luck! Just accomplished one of the finest flights on record. Started from up here; skimmed over the Channel to Boulogne; circled round the cathedral—such a clear day; we could watch the whole flight with field-glasses—came gaily back without a stop; was making for the cliff again, when a cross-current caught him; something went wrong with the steering-gear; and down it goes, with a plunge, head first into the sea."

"And the—er—occupant?" inquired the Professor.

"The aeronaut? Ah, he didn't fall clear, worse luck, or they could soon have fished him out. He stuck to his seat and his wheel, and fell smash in among his wires. They are trying to extricate him now. Bad luck, poor chap! Such a sport."

"Do you know his name?" asked the Professor, peering down at the waiting crowd which lined the beach.

"Guy Chelsea," said the man. "And I give you my word, he was the finest, pluckiest young amateur we had among the airmen."

Then Christobel's heart began to beat again, and her limbs seemed to regain the power to move.

"He is mine," she said. "I must go to him. He is my own Little Boy Blue." And she began to run along the Leas toward the stone steps which zigzag down to the shore.

She heard the Professor running after her.

"Ann," he called, "Ann! Stay! This is—most—unnecessary!"

She flew on.

"At least take the lift!" bawled the Professor.

She hurried on and reached the steps, pausing an instant to glance back.

The Professor had stopped at the lift, and was waving to her with his umbrella.

She could never remember running down those steps. In what seemed but a moment from the time she reached them, she found herself stumbling painfully down the steep slope of shingle to the water's edge.

The lift, bearing the Professor, had just begun to crawl down the face of the cliff. She could see him gesticulating through the glass windows.

The crowd on the shore, chiefly composed of rough men, was thickest round the base of a wide stone breakwater, jutting out into the sea. On this break-water stood an empty stretcher. A coast-

120

guardsman marched up and down, keeping the crowd off the breakwater.

Christobel reached the outskirts of the crowd, and could get no farther.

"Please let me through," she said. "I belong to him. He is mine."

They turned and looked at her.

"She's 'is mother," said a voice. "Let 'er through."

"Mother be blowed!" said another voice, hoarsely. "Get out! She's 'is wife."

"Yes," she cried eagerly. "Yes! Oh, do let me through! I am his wife."

Suddenly she knew it was true. The Boy's great love had made her his wife. Had he not said: "You and I are one, Christobel; eternally, indissolubly one. You will find it out, when it is too late"?

The crowd parted, making a way for her, straight to the foot of the breakwater.

She mounted it, and walked towards the empty stretcher.

The coast-guardsman confronted her.

"He is mine," she said, quietly. "I have the right to be here."

The man saluted, in respectful silence.

She stood gazing out to where the crowd of boats hovered about the great insect with broken wings.

The sea gleamed golden in the sunset.

One boat, larger than the rest, slowly detached itself from the general mêlée, pulling with measured stroke toward the breakwater.

Something lay very still in the bow, covered with a sail-cloth.

Two coast-guardsmen rowed; one steered.

The boat came toward the breakwater, in a shaft of sunlight.

Christobel turned to the man beside her.

"Is there any hope?" she asked.

"'Fraid not, lady. My mate just signalled: all U P."

"Ah!" she said, looking wide-eyed into his face. "Ah!—But there must be pioneers."

The coast-guardsman turned and walked toward the crowd.

"She's 'is wife, men," he said, with a jerk of his thumb over his shoulder. "She's 'is wife; yet when I told her it was all U P, she said: 'There must be pioneers.'"

The crowd of roughs doffed their caps.

The boat drew slowly nearer.

Then she saw the Professor, hurrying down the shingle, waving his umbrella.

He must not come yet.

She advanced to the shore end of the breakwater, and spoke to the crowd.

"Please," she said, "oh, please, if possible, prevent that gentleman from reaching the breakwater."

They turned, and saw the advancing figure of the Professor, flurried and irate.

"'Ullo, Bill," cried a voice. "She says: Don't let the old bloke through."

They passed the word from one to the other. "Don't let the old bloke through." They closed the outer ranks, standing shoulder to shoulder. The Professor's umbrella waved wildly on the outskirts.

She moved along the breakwater. Yes, that was it. "Don't let the old bloke through." She had never used such a word in her life before, but it just met the needs of the case. "Don't let the old bloke through."

The boat drew nearer.

A bugle, away up on the cliff, sounded the call to arms.

"Little Boy Blue, come blow me your horn! The cow's in the meadow; the sheep, in the corn. Where is the boy who looks after the sheep? Ah, dear God! Where is the Boy? Where is the Boy? Where is the Boy?—He's under the sailcloth—fast asleep."

The boat drew nearer. She could hear the measured plash of the oars; the rhythmic rattle of the rowlocks. They advanced, to the beat of the words in her brain.

"There must—be pion—eers! Don't let the old bloke through. Oh, where is the boy who looks after the sheep? He's under the sail-cloth, fast asleep."

The boat drew level with the breakwater, grating against it.

"Under the sail-cloth, Boy dear; under the sail-cloth—fast asleep."

123

Tenderly, carefully, they lifted their burden. As the boat rocked, and their feet shuffled beneath the weight, she closed her eyes. When she opened them once more, the quiet Thing under the sail-cloth lay upon the stretcher. Every man within sight stood silent and bareheaded.

The bugle on the cliff sounded: "lights out."

The golden shaft of sunlight died from off the sea.

Then she came forward, and knelt beside her Boy.

Suddenly she understood the cry of anguish wrung from the loving heart of a woman at a tomb: "Tell me where thou hast laid Him, and I will take Him away!" Oh, faithful heart of woman, alike through all the ages; ready, with superhuman effort, to prove a limitless love and a measureless grief!

She knelt beside the stretcher, and lifted the sail-cloth.

Yes, it was the Boy—her own Little Boy Blue.

His curly hair was matted with blood and salt water. There was a deep gash across his temple, from the ear, right up into the hair His eyes were closed; but his lips smiled, triumphant. "There must be pioneers! Every good life given, advances the cause." "Yes, Little Boy Blue. But has it ever struck you, that, if you marry, your wife will most probably want you to give up flying; not being able to bear that a man who was her ALL, should do these things?" She lifted the sail-cloth quite away, and stood looking down upon him, so shattered, yet so beautiful, in his triumphant sleep.

Suddenly her arm was seized from behind. She turned.

The Professor had succeeded in pushing his way through the

124

crowd, and in mounting the breakwater. His cravat was awry; his top-hat was on the back of his head. He looked at her through his glasses, in amazed indignation.

"Christobel," he said, "this is no place for you. Come away at once. Do you hear? I bid you come with me at once."

The only thing she really minded was that his hat was on, in the presence of her Dead.

She could not free her arm from the grip of the Professor.

She turned and pointed to the stretcher, with her left hand.

"My place is here," she said, clearly and deliberately. "I have the right to be here. This is all a fearful nightmare, from which we are bound before long to wake. But meanwhile, I tell you plainly—as I ought to have told you before—this is the body of the man I love."

At that moment, one of the crowd, springing on to the breakwater behind the Professor, struck off his hat with a cane. It fell into the sea.

The Professor let go her arm, and turned to see who had perpetrated the outrage, and whether the hat could be recovered.

Then she bent over the stretcher.

"Boy dear," she whispered, in tones of ineffable tenderness; "this is where they have laid you; but I will take you away."

She put her arms beneath the body; then, with an almost superhuman effort, lifted it, and gathered it to her. It felt limp and broken. The head fell heavily against her breast. The blood and salt-water soaked through her thin muslin blouse. But she held him, and would not let him go. "I will take him away," she whispered; "I will take him away."

She knew she was losing her reason, but she had known that, ever since she first looked down from the top of the cliff, and saw the broken wings floating on the sea. Now, with her Boy in her arms, her one idea was to get away from the Professor; away from the coast-guardsmen; away from the crowd.

Turning her back upon the beach, she staggered along the breakwater, toward the open sea.

"I will take him away," she repeated; "I will take him away."

Then her foot slipped. She still held the Boy, but she felt herself falling.

She closed her eyes.

She never knew which she struck first, the stone breakwater, or the sea— —

THE SEVENTH DAY

THE STONE IS ROLLED AWAY

When Christobel recovered consciousness and opened her eyes, she found herself in bed, in her own room, at home.

Martha bent over her.

The morning light entered dimly, through closed curtains.

In dumb anguish of mind, she looked up into Martha's grim old face.

"Tell me where you have laid him," she said, "and I will take him away."

Martha snorted.

"I've laid your tea-tray on the table beside your bed, Miss," she said; "and when you 'ave finished with it, I will take it away."

Whereupon, Martha lumbered to the large bow-window, drew back all the curtains with a vigorous clatter of brass rings, and let in a blaze of morning sunshine.

Christobel lay quite still, trying to collect her thoughts.

One of her pillows was clasped tightly in her arms.

She lifted her left hand, and looked at it.

No ring encircled the third finger.

127

"Martha," she called, softly.

Martha loomed large at the side of the bed.

"What is to-day?"

"Wednesday, Miss," replied Martha, too much surprised to be contemptuous.

"Martha—where is Mr. Chelsea?"

"Lord only knows," said Martha, tragically.

"Martha—is he—living?"

"Living?" repeated Martha, deliberately. Then she smiled, her crooked smile. "Living don't express it, Miss Christobel. Lively's more like it, when Mr. Guy is concerned. And I reckon, wherever 'e is, e's makin' things lively somewhere for somebody. You don't look quite the thing this morning, Miss. Sit up and take your tea."

She sat up, loosing the pillow out of her arms—the pillow which had been, first her Little Boy Blue, as she drew him to her in the darkness; then the dead body of Guy Chelsea, as she lifted it on the breakwater.

She took her tea from Martha's hand, and drank it quickly. She wanted Martha to go.

It was Wednesday! Then the Boy had left her only the day before yesterday. His telegram had come last night. The Professor's proposal had not yet reached her.

Martha lifted the tray and departed.

Then Christobel Charteris rose, and stood at her open window, in

128

the morning sunlight. She looked out upon the mulberry-tree and the long vista of soft turf; in the dim distance, the postern gate in the old red wall—his paradise, and hers.

She lifted her beautiful arms above her head. The loose sleeves of her nightdress fell away, baring them to the elbows. She might have stood, in her noble development of face and form, for a splendid statue of hope and praise.

"Ah, dear God!" she breathed, "is it indeed true? Is it possible? Is my Boy alive? And am I free—free to be his alone? Am I free to give him all he wants, free to be all he needs?"

She stood long at the window motionless, realizing the mental adjustment which had come to her during the strenuous hours of the night.

Her dream had taught her one great lesson: That under no circumstances whatever, can it be right for a woman to marry one man, while with her whole being she loves another. Love is Lord of all. Love reigns paramount. No expectations, past or present, based on friendship or gratitude; no sense of duty or obligations of any kind could make a marriage right, if, in view of that marriage, Love had to stand by with broken wings.

She felt quite sure, now, that she could never marry the Professor; and humbly she thanked God for opening her eyes to the wrong she had contemplated, before it was too late.

But there still remained the difficult prospect of having to disappoint a man she esteemed so highly; a man who had been led to believe she cared for him, and had waited years for him; a man who, for years, had set his heart upon her. This was a heavy stone, and it lay right in the path of perfect bliss which she longed to tread with her Little Boy Blue.

Who should roll it away?

Could she feel free to take happiness with the Boy, if she had disappointed and crushed a deeply sensitive nature which trusted her?

She dressed, and went down to the breakfast-room, her soul filled, in spite of perplexities, with a radiance of glad thanksgiving.

Martha and Jenkins came in to prayers. Martha had now taken to curling all her wisps. She appeared with many frizzled ringlets, kept in place by invisible pins.

Martha always came in to prayers, as if she were marching at the head of a long row of men and maids. Jenkins followed meekly, placing his chair at what would have been the tail of Martha's imaginary retinue. According to the triumphant dignity of Martha's entry, Jenkins placed his chair near or far away. Martha was in great form to-day. Jenkins sat almost at the door. If the door-bell rang during prayers, the first ring was tacitly ignored; but if it rang again, Martha signed to Jenkins, who tiptoed reverently out, and answered it. No matter how early in the morning's devotions the interruption occurred, Jenkins never considered it etiquette to return. Miss Charteris used to dread a duet alone with Martha. She always became too intensely conscious of herself and of Martha, to be uplifted as usual by the inspired words of Bible and Prayer-book. The presence of Jenkins at once constituted a congregation.

On this particular morning, no interruptions occurred.

The portion for the day chanced to be the scene at the empty tomb, in the early dawn of that first Easter Day, as given by Saint Mark.

130

The quiet voice vibrated with unusual emotion as Miss Charteris read:

"And very early in the morning, the first day of the week, they came unto the sepulchre at the rising of the sun. And they said among themselves, Who shall roll us away the stone from the door of the sepulchre? And when they looked, they saw that the stone was rolled away: for it was very great."

Christobel Charteris paused. She seemed to see the shore at Dovercourt, and the brave little figure struggling to carry the heavy stone; and, later on when the cannon-ball lay safely in the castle court-yard, Little Boy Blue standing erect, with lifted cap, and shining eyes, a picture of faith triumphant.

"I have prayed for thee, that thy faith fail not."

How far were the happenings of this strange night owing to that dead mother's prayers; and to the Boy's unfailing faith, even through these hard days?

Miss Charteris could read no farther. She closed the Bible. "Let us pray," she said, and turned to the Collect for the week.

"O God, Whose never-failing providence ordereth all things both in heaven and earth: We humbly beseech Thee to put away from us all hurtful things, and to give us those things which be profitable for us; through Jesus Christ our Lord. Amen."

On the breakfast-table, beside her plate, lay the Professor's letter. She had known it would be there.

She poured out her coffee and buttered her toast.

Then she opened the letter.

131

"My dear Ann"— —

After the nightmare through which she had just passed, this beginning scarcely surprised her. She glanced back at the envelope to make quite sure it was addressed to herself; then read on. It was dated the evening before, from the Professor's rooms in College.

"MY DEAR ANN,—I regret to have been unable to look in upon you this evening, on my return from town, and my duties will keep me from paying you a visit until to-morrow, in the late afternoon. Hence this letter.

"Needless to say, I have been thinking over, carefully, the remarkable statement you saw fit to make to me, concerning the feelings and expectations of our young friend. It came to me as a genuine surprise. I have always looked upon our friendship as purely Platonic; based entirely upon the intellectual enjoyment we found in pursuing our classical studies together.

"I admit, I cannot bring myself to contemplate matrimony with much enthusiasm.

"At the same time, your feeling in the matter being so strong, and my sense of gratitude toward my late friend, a thing never to be forgotten; if you are quite sure, Ann—and I confess it seems to me altogether incredible—that our young friend entertains, toward me, feelings which will mean serious disappointment to her, if I fail—"

This brought the letter to the bottom of the first page.

Without reading any farther, Miss Charteris folded it, and replaced it in the envelope.

The indignant blood had mounted to the roots of her soft fair hair. But already, in her heart, sounded a song of wondering praise.

132

"And when they looked, they saw that the stone was rolled away: for it was very great."

The iron gate of the front garden swung open. Hurried steps flew up the path. Emma, poor soul, had been told to fly; and Emma had flown. She almost fell into the arms of Jenkins, as he opened the hall door.

The note with which Emma had run, at a speed which was now causing her "such a stitch as never was," came from Miss Ann, and was marked "urgent" and "immediate."

The corners of Christobel's proud mouth curved into a quiet smile as she took it from the salver. She had expected this note.

"Take Emma downstairs, Jenkins," she said. "Ask Martha to give her a cup of coffee, and an egg, if she fancies it. Tell Emma, I wish her to sit down comfortably and rest. The answer to this note will be ready in about half an hour; not before."

Miss Charteris finished her coffee and toast, poured out a fresh cup, and took some marmalade. She did not hurry over her breakfast.

When she had quite finished, she rose, and walked over to the writing-table. She sat down, opened her blotter, took paper and envelopes; found a pen, and tried it.

Then she opened Miss Ann's letter, marked "urgent" and "immediate."

"SWEETEST CHILD" (wrote Miss Ann)—"See what Kenrick has done! We—you and I—so understand his dear absent-minded ways. He wrote this letter to you last night, and, owing to his natural emotion and tension of mind, addressed it to me! Needless to say, I have read only the opening sentences. Darling Christobel, you will, I feel sure, overlook the very natural mistake, and not allow it in any way to affect your answer to my brother's proposal. Remember how difficult it is for great minds to be accurate in the small details of daily life. I have known Kenrick to put two spoonfuls of mustard into a cup of coffee, stir it round, and drink it, quite unaware that anything was wrong—I have indeed! See how our dear Professor needs a wife!

"I feel quite foolishly anxious this morning. Do send me one line of assurance that all is well. You cannot but be touched by my brother's letter. From beginning to end, it breathes the faithful devotion of a lifetime. Do not misunderstand the natural reticence of one wholly unaccustomed to the voicing of sentiment. I only wish you could hear all he says to me!"

Then followed a few prayers and devout allusions to Providence— which brought a stern look to the face of Miss Charteris—and, with a whiff of effusive sentiment, Ann Harvey closed her epistle.

An open letter from the Professor to herself was enclosed; but this, Christobel quietly laid aside.

She took pen and paper, and wrote at once the note for which Emma waited.

"DEAR ANN,—I enclose a letter from your brother which came, addressed to me, this morning, but was evidently intended for you. I have read only the first page, which was quite sufficient to make the true state of affairs perfectly clear to me.

"Providence has indeed interposed, by means of the Professor's absent-minded ways, to prevent the wrecking of three lives—mine, your brother's, and that of the man I love; to whom I shall be betrothed before the day is over.

"I shall not tell the Professor that I have seen a portion of his letter to you. I think we owe it to him not to do so. He has always been a true and honourable friend to me.

"Yours, "C. C."

When Emma had duly departed with this letter and enclosure, Miss Charteris breathed more freely. She had been afraid lest, in her righteous indignation, in her consciousness of the terrible mischief so nearly wrought, she should write too strongly to Miss Ann, thus causing her unnecessary pain.

It was quite impossible, to the fine generosity of a nature such as that of Christobel Charteris, really to understand the mean, self-centred, unscrupulous dishonesty of an action such as this of Miss Ann's. From the calm heights whereon she walked, such small-minded selfishness of motive did not come within her field of vision. She could never bring herself to believe worse of Miss Ann than that, in some incomprehensible way, she had laboured under a delusion regarding herself and the Professor.

Miss Ann disposed of, she turned to the Professor's letter.

It was not the letter of her dream, by any means; nor was it the letter she had sometimes dreamed he would write.

It was straightforward and simple; and, holding the key to the situation, she could read between the lines a certain amount of dismayed surprise, which made her heartily sorry for her old friend.

The Professor touched on their long friendship, his regard for her parents, his sincere admiration for herself; their unity of interests and congeniality of tastes; his sudden change of fortunes; quoted a

135

little Greek, a little Sanskrit, and a little Persian; then, fortified by these familiar aids to the emotions, offered her marriage, in valiant and unmistakable terms.

Christobel's heart stood still as she realized that not one word in that letter would have revealed to her the true state of the case. Truly, under Providence, she had cause to bless the Professor's "dear absent-minded ways."

As she took pen and paper to reply to his letter, her heart felt very warm toward her old friend. She gave him full credit for the effort with which he had done what he had been led to consider was the right thing toward her.

"MY DEAR PROFESSOR" (she wrote),—"I rejoice to hear of your good fortune. It is well indeed when the great thinkers of the world are rendered independent of all anxious taking of thought as to what they shall eat, or what they shall drink, or wherewithal they shall be clothed. I like to think of you, my friend, as now set completely free from all mundane cares; able to give your undivided attention to the work you love.

"I appreciate, more than I can say, the kind proposition concerning myself, which you make in your letter. I owe it to our friendship to tell you quite frankly that I feel, and have long felt, how great an honour it would be for any woman to be in a position so to administer your household as to set you completely free for your great intellectual pursuits.

"But marriage would mean more than this, and our long friendship emboldens me to say that I should grieve to see you—owing perhaps to pressure or advice from others—burden your life with family ties for which you surely do not yourself feel any special inclination.

136

"And, now, my friend, I must not close my letter without telling you how great a happiness has come into my lonely life. I am about to marry a man whom—" Miss Charteris paused, and looked through the open window to the softly moving leaves of the old mulberry-tree. A gleam of amusement shone in her eyes, curving her lips into a tender smile. The Boy seemed beside her, slapping his knee and rocking with merriment at the way she was about to bewilder Miss Ann and the Professor—"a man whom I have known and loved for over twenty years.

"I am sure you will wish me joy, dear Professor.

"Believe me, always,
"Gratefully and affectionately yours,
"CHRISTOBEL CHARTERIS."

She rang the bell, and sent the answer to the Professor's letter, by Jenkins. She could not wait for the slow medium of the post. She could not let him remain another hour in the belief that, in order to save her from disappointment, he was compelled to marry Christobel Charteris.

She stood at the breakfast-room window, and watched Jenkins as he hurried down the garden with the note. Going by the lane, and taking a short cut across the fields, he would reach the Professor's rooms in a quarter of an hour. Until then, life was somewhat intolerable.

The proud blood mantled again over the face, the strong sweet beauty of which the Boy so loved. Her letter to the Professor had not been easy to write. She had had to be true to herself, and true to him, in the light of what she knew to be his real feeling in the matter; bearing in mind that before long he would almost certainly learn from Miss Ann that she had replied to his proposal after

137

having read his sentiments on the subject, so candidly expressed on the first page of his letter to his sister.

To relieve her mind, after this intricate whirl of cross-correspondence, she took up the Daily Graphic, and opened it, casually turning the pages.

Suddenly there looked out at her from the central page, the merry, handsome, daring face of her own Little Boy Blue. He was seated in his flying-machine steering-wheel in hand, looking out from among many wires. His cap was on the back of his head, his bright eyes looked straight into hers; his firm young lips, parted in a smile, seemed to say; "I jolly well mean to do it!" It was the very picture she had seen in the Professor's Daily Mirror, in her dream of the night before. Below was an account of the flight from Folkestone which he was about to attempt.

Then she remembered, with a shock of realization, that the flight across the Channel, round Boulogne Cathedral and back, was to take place on that very day. His telegram, of the night before, had said: "I am going to do a big fly to-morrow. Wish me luck." Ah, what if it ended as she had seen it end in her dream: great broken wings; a mass of tangled wire; and the Boy—her Boy—with matted hair, and wounded head, asleep beneath the sailcloth!

Her heart stood still.

With their perfect joy so near its fulfilment, she could not let him take the risk. Was there time to stop him?

She looked at the paper. The start was for 2 p.m. It was now eleven o'clock.

She remembered his last words: "When you want me and send— why, I will come from the other end of the world."

She never quite knew how she reached the telegraph-office. It seemed almost as dreamlike as her flight from the top to the bottom of the Folkestone cliffs. But it was not a dream this time; it was desperate reality.

Why do people always break the points of the pencils hanging from strings in the telegraph-offices? Surely it is possible to write a telegram without stubbing off the pencil, and leaving it in that condition, for the next person in a hurry.

She flew from compartment to compartment, and at last produced her own pencil, and wrote her telegram in the final section of the row, independent of official broken points.

"Do not fly to-day. Come to me. I want you.
"Christobel."

She addressed it to the hotel from which he had telegraphed on the previous day; but added to the address: "If not there, send immediately to aviation sheds." She had no idea what to call the places, but this sounded well, and seemed an intuition, or an unconscious recollection of some remark of the Boy's.

She handed it over the counter. "Please see that it goes through at once," she said.

The clerk knew her. "Yes, Miss Charteris," he replied. He began reading the message aloud, but almost immediately stopped, and checked the words off silently. He glanced at the clock. "It should be there before noon, Miss Charteris," he said.

He did not look at her, as he passed her the stamps. He had long thought her one of the finest women who stepped in and out of the post-office. He had never expected to see her hands tremble. And fancy any woman—even she—being able to tell Guy Chelsea not to fly! He had a bet on, about that flight, with an enthusiastic backer of Chelsea's. He was glad he had taken the odds against its coming off, before seeing this wire. But—after all! It is easy enough to ask a chap not to fly; but——

He took up a copy of the Daily Mirror, and looked at the brave smiling face. "I jolly well mean to do it!" the young aeronaut seemed to be saying. The clerk laughed, and shook his head. "Hurry up that wire," he called to the operator. Then he jingled the loose change in his pockets. "I wonder," he said.

During the hours which followed, Christobel Charteris knew suspense.

Perhaps that strong, self-contained nature could never have fully sounded the depths of its own surrender, without those hours of uncertainty, when nothing stood between her and the man she loved, but the possibility that her telegram would fail to reach him; that he would carry out his dangerous flight; that disaster and death would overtake him and wrest him from her, and that he would die—Guy Chelsea would die—without ever knowing of the cup of bliss she was now ready, with utterly loving hand, to hold to his lips.

Having sent her message, there was nothing more she could do, and the burden of inaction seemed almost too great a weight to carry, during the hours which must elapse, before his coming could turn uncertainty into assurance; restlessness, into peace.

It did not occur to her, as a possibility, that Guy Chelsea would elect to fly, after receiving her request. She knew her slightest wish would be law to the Boy's tender loyalty; and though he knew nothing of her cause for anxiety, nor of the complete change of circumstances since he left her, not forty-eight hours before, she felt sure he would not fly; she felt certain he would come—if—if the message reached him in time.

At two o'clock it came to her, with overwhelming certainty, that her message had not reached him, and that he had started on his flight. She seemed to see the great wings mounting—mounting; then skimming over the sea. She almost heard the hum he had so often described—the hum of the giant insect on which the bird-man flew.

Her own Little Boy Blue was flying through space. O God, what might not any minute be bringing! He had said: "One never expects those things to happen, and when they do happen, it's over so quickly that there is no time for expectation." Was it happening now? Was it going to be over so quickly, that her cup of bliss would be dashed from her lips untasted? Was she to lose her all, because of a cross-current or a twisted wire?

She was walking up and down the garden now, and paused beside the chair in which she had sat when he had said, only seven days ago: "It was always you I wanted; not your niece. Good heavens! How can you have thought it was Mollie, when it was you—you— just only you, all the time?" And she, half-laughing at him, had asked: "Is this a proposal?"

"My ALL," she said. "Oh, Boy dear, my ALL. If I lose you, I lose my ALL."

She walked on slowly, moving to the repetition of those words. It seemed a comfort to repeat the great fact that, at last, he was this to her. Surely it would reach him, by some sort of wireless telegraphy through space. Surely it would control cross-currents, keep propellers acting as they should; steering-gear from twisting.

141

"O God, he is my ALL—he is my ALL!"

The afternoon sun began to glint through the trees.

The jolly little "what-d'-you-call-'ems" lifted pale anxious faces to the sky.

Clocks all around chimed the hour of four.

Suddenly her limbs weakened. She could walk no longer.

She sank into a chair, beneath the mulberry-tree.

In a few minutes Jenkins would bring out tea. Would Martha have arranged a tea such as the Boy loved, with cups for two, hot buttered-toast and explosive buns?

What a boy he was, at heart—this man who had won her; what a gay, laughter-loving boy!

She lay back, very still, under the mulberry-tree, and lived again through each of the Boy's days, from the first to the sixth.

She kept her eyes closed. The sunlight, glinting through the mulberry leaves, fell in bright patches on her white gown, and on her soft golden hair.

The garden was very still. All nature seemed waiting with the heart that waited.

"Little Boy Blue, come blow me your horn!"

"I shall blow it all right on the seventh day," the Boy had said; "and when I do, you will hear it."

This was the seventh day.

Suddenly the horn of a motor tooted loudly in the lane.

She rose, her hands clasped upon her breast, and stood waiting

A shaft of golden sunlight streamed down the garden, and seemed to focus on the postern gate.

Then the gate swung open and the Boy came in, slamming it behind him. She saw him coming up the lawn toward her, bareheaded; the sunlight in his shining eyes.

"I couldn't wait for trains," he shouted. "I came by motor. And I jolly well exceeded the speed-limit all the way!"

She moved a few steps to meet him.

"Boy dear," she said, "you always exceed all speed-limits. It is a way you have. Exceed them as much as you like, so long as I am with you when you do it. But—oh, my Little Boy Blue!—don't fly again; for, if you fall and break your wings, indeed you will break my heart."

In a moment she was sobbing on his breast, her arms flung around him. There was nothing broken or limp about his strong young body, pulsating with life.

He put his arms about her, holding her in a clasp of close possessive tenderness.

He did not yet understand what had happened; but he knew the great gift he desired had been given him. He waited for her to speak.

She lifted her face to his.

"Guy," she said; "ah, take me, hold me, keep me! I am altogether your own. I will explain to you fully, by and by. The stone was very great; but lo, as we reached it, the Angel of the Lord had rolled it away.... No other man has a shadow of claim over me. I am free to say, to the only man I have ever really loved: Take me; I am yours. Oh, Boy! I am altogether yours."

He bent over her.

The sweet proud lips were parted in utter surrender, and lifted to his.

He paused—just for one exquisite moment, of realization.

She waited his kiss with closed eyes, so she did not see the radiance of his face, as he looked up to the blue sky, flecked with fleeting white clouds. But she heard the voice, which from that hour was to make the music of her life:

"Thank the Lord," said Little Boy Blue.

Then—he kissed her.

"And the evening and the morning were the seventh day."